Stormy Cliff

Luke Temple

Pen Press Publishers Ltd

www.stormycliff.co.uk

First published in Great Britain by
Pen Press Publishers Ltd
25 Eastern Place
Brighton
BN2 1GJ

ISBN13: 978-1-906206-94-9

Printed and bound in the UK

A catalogue record of this book is available from
the British Library

From an idea by Luke Temple and Kieran Burling
Cover and Illustrations by Jessica Chiba

A Story from Thistlewick Island

Book 1

For the treasures in my life,
whom I am lucky to have.

Prologue

1880

Many would have found the rough seas that the Tormenta faced a daunting challenge, but for Captain Traiton and his crew it was just an average night. Treacherous waters always seemed to follow them and like any half decent pirates they loved it. But these weren't just half decent pirates, they were the best, hated by many, feared by even more – the scourge of the seas, and they knew it. What they didn't know was that tonight was to be the last they would spend sailing in the Tormenta.

The wind howled as the waves crashed against the dense wooden sides of the ship. It was heavy with gold from the pirates' last victory against a British Navy vessel. The crew were merry from the amount of rum consumed and Captain Traiton was the only person onboard with a clear head. He liked to see his men happy, but someone needed to keep an eye out for dangers, from both nature and other ships.

'Mr Brownjohn, pull yourself together and tell me where we're headed,' he bellowed to his second in command, who was swaying next to him, holding a large bottle half full of rum.

Brownjohn grabbed a map from his pocket after taking a violent swig of the rum and moved over to a swinging lantern so that he could see it properly. He studied the map closely.

'We're a couple of miles off a small island carrying the name of Thistlewick, Capt'n.'

'Hmmm. I don't recognise it. Ring any bells?'

'Any what, sir?'

'Any bells!' Traiton shouted over the noise of a wave crashing into the ship.

'Oh no, I've not heard tell of it.'

'Does it look promising?'

'Seems pretty deserted, and this map's up to date.'

'We'll pass on by then. Head north, Brownjohn, I want to land somewhere lucrative before daybreak.'

'Right you are, Capt'n.'

Brownjohn staggered to the wheel and with a big tug turned it powerfully around. The Tormenta moved an unsteady ninety degrees and slowly battled northwards against the growing waves on its endless journey to even more riches.

Up and down, to and fro, the rhythm of ship against wave that left so many stomachs unsettled gave peace to Captain Traiton's heart. He loved the sea and the gold; he was excited by battle and revelled in victory. This made him the perfect pirate, he thought, as he stood tall on deck, smelling and tasting the sea as it crashed around him.

As the Tormenta moved forwards, a mist began to form around it. Although this usually gave protection from enemy craft, it was now, in the growing darkness, starting to trap the ship. With the impact of a huge wave came the roar of the pirates from below deck.

His eyes already fogged over from hours of drinking, the mist wasn't helping Brownjohn to steer the ship.

'I've never seen the weather this bad before,' he muttered to himself.

'You've obviously never been in these parts then?' said Traiton heartily, overhearing his second in command. 'I've seen much worse than this. It'll pass soon enough.'

But it didn't, and continued to get worse as the waves tore at the ship and the ghostly mist soared around it, circling its prey.

Wearily they moved on, and a few of the crew came up on deck to secure the rigging. As they were doing so there was a sudden ear-splitting crunch. The men at the side of the ship shot backwards in shock, but Captain Traiton instinctively ran to the source of the noise and looked over the side. He froze for a second, thinking what he could do as fear filled him. Then he shouted:

'We've been hit! We're going down!'

Stormy Cliff

Dear Zoe,

To say thank you for helping me
with my second book, I give
you my first!
You're a star!

Luke   Sept 09

Chapter 1

The Present Day – The Davies Family's Morning Routine

Ben Davies liked his morning routine. It was quite rushed and always a push to get out of the house on time, but at least it kept him on his toes. He wasn't the tidiest of eleven year olds at the best of times, and perhaps the speed at which everything took place in the thirty minutes before school added to this image. Ben wasn't really worried about how he presented himself – he had scruffy dark hair, a thin figure and an interesting dress sense, but he didn't look in the mirror so this didn't bother him. His twin sister Harriet, on the other hand, liked to take things at a steady pace and everything had to be just perfect before she even considered putting a foot out of the front door. Because of this the pair looked quite different for twins, but they didn't mind.

The Davies family was facing a tough time at the moment. Ben and Harriet's father had been ill for some time and was only just starting to recover. Their mother was struggling to look after them all while holding down a steady job and bringing in just enough money to keep them afloat. She always seemed to have enough time to support them in their hobbies and at school though – no one knew quite how she managed it.

The family lived on the island of Thistlewick, which was surrounded by rough seas all year round. A large part of Thistlewick was uninhabited due to a vast, dark forest at its centre, and there was only room for one village on the south of the island. As well as a rather typical church, there was the small school that Ben and Harriet attended, a two-manned police station, a quaint market and a miniature fishing fleet. The reachable parts of the north of the island, past the dark forest, were mainly farmers' fields. The village was a compact community, the kind where everyone is your neighbour and no one feels excluded. All the Davies family enjoyed living in a place like this.

It was Monday 12th November, and when all the alarms went off around the seven o'clock region, the family awoke to an overcast, blustery morning. After the bathroom run, they all had breakfast in the parents' bedroom because the children wanted to spend time with their dad, who wasn't allowed to move out of bed. This was always the time when the family was closest, sitting on and around the big double bed while eating a quick round of toast.

'Well I hope all our days fare well,' said Mrs Davies, passing round three pots of jam and one of peanut butter to Ben. 'And I hope you two don't get too bored at school.' She looked lovingly at Ben and Harriet in turn. She was very proud of them for being there for their father.

'I can safely say that they won't get as bored as I will,' chipped in Mr Davies, who always enjoyed the family's morning get-togethers.

'I'd take a day in bed over school any time!' Ben exclaimed, staring at the grey sky and rough sea out of the bedroom window. He wasn't joking.

'Oh, Harriet dear, don't forget to ask Catherine if her mum needs help with the salads on Thursday.' Mrs Davies was about to dig into her next side-project, catering for the wedding of a couple who were new to the island.

'Will do, Mum,' replied Harriet, busy spreading strawberry jam neatly over her toast.

'You do enough as it is, dear,' Mr Davies said to his wife. 'I don't know how you fit everything in on top of looking after me and the children.'

'I manage, Stan, I manage.'

They ate their toast and drank up the freshly squeezed orange juice as the minutes ticked by, until there was a sharp knock on the front door.

'Crikey, that must be the post.' Mrs Davies looked to the clock. 'And look at the time! You two had better hurry up and pack your bags. Don't want to be late for school. Remember your coats today, you'll need them.'

And so another morning ritual began with Mrs Davies standing by the door as Ben and Harriet prepared for school. Despite being a perfectionist, Harriet arrived by her mum first, her long hair combed straight, her uniform perfectly presentable and her bag efficiently packed. After waiting for several minutes, Mrs Davies began to call out, 'Hurry up, Ben, or you'll be late!' at regular intervals, until Ben rushed up to the door, hair uncombed, uniform untucked and bag slung loosely over one shoulder. Both children grabbed their coats from the hook behind the door and after a quick goodbye kiss they were gone, leaving their mum to get ready for work.

* * *

The journey to school took the twins along a couple of winding coastal paths, past the white houses with granite grey roofs that were dotted loosely around rolling grass and thick hedges. They had made this journey on their own for the last few years, Ben confident and independent and Harriet happy as long as he was there to walk with. Despite being rather different in character, they were closer than most brother and sister pairings.

Quite often on their journey they would stop and gaze out to the deep blue sea, curious about what was out there, or watch the fishermen in the harbour rigging up their boats ready for a day on the waves. This morning there was a strong, bitter wind that blew spray from the tall waves onto the island, so Ben and Harriet didn't stop and instead walked as quickly as possible, trying to avoid being blown over. They could taste the salt from the spray blowing into them in their every breath.

'I love this type of weather,' Ben shouted in the direction of his sister. His hair was becoming more and more windswept.

'It does fit Thistlewick well, doesn't it,' Harriet replied, her voice hitting the wind. She had her hood up and her coat tightly wrapped around her, so that all that could be seen was a pale, freckly face and two hazel eyes.

'I'm glad we'll be inside today though, but Stormy Cliff will probably be rattling like a skeleton in a cage.'

'Yes, and there's the holes in the roof now, so I hope it doesn't rain.'

Stormy Cliff was the small school on the island, which the children had attended for most of their lives. It had become gradually more run down in recent years.

As they passed the harbour one of the fishermen, Mr Gailsborough – a mad but lovable boater, whose heavy wrinkles showed the depths of the sea he sailed in – waved at them and they returned the gesture. It was incredible how the weather didn't seem to bother the fishermen – they always went out to sea, come sunshine and blue skies or heavy rain and stormy waves. Perhaps they were fearless, or maybe they just knew the sea well.

Moving expertly along the path, Ben and Harriet's feet guided them away from puddles and holes in the ground as their eyes focused in front of them. They didn't know a lot of the island that well, but this path they could walk blindfolded. As it started to widen out, they turned right onto the main track, taking them away from the sea, through a row of terraced houses and into the heart of the village. Here the wind wasn't as bad because they were protected by the buildings around them. On the whole the village was quaint and peaceful, fitting the close-knit, relaxed community. The layout was simple and comfortably spread out, with a very natural feel to it.

As the children passed over the village green and arrived at the rusty side gates of Stormy Cliff, the wind seemed to have ceased completely and they looked back over a magnificent view of the choppy sea, taking it all in before turning around to face their school.

The impression you would get if you walked up to Stormy Cliff School for the first time was of a building once cared for greatly, which had recently been neglected and was now falling into ruins. It would never have been considered an impressive or imposing building, but it had a solid structure that had battled against the weather for centuries. The roof was missing many tiles and there were obvious holes in it now; the windows were grimy and dark and the walls were crumbling in the gaps that hadn't seen paint for many years. All in all the building symbolised the current state of the school well.

'Another boring day ahead of us then, sis,' Ben sighed, looking forlorn. He didn't look forward to going to school like he used to, it just wasn't fun any more.

'You shouldn't be so negative, Ben. You never know what

could happen today. Mr Harris might start something new.'
Harriet always tried to be positive about school.

'Whatever it is, it won't be fun or exciting.'

'That's not Mr Harris's fault though. I'm sure he'll try his best.'

'Yep, I'm sure he will.'

Ben flicked the latch on the gate and let Harriet push it open. It groaned in its old age when the rusty hinges turned as it opened and closed, letting the twins through. They tramped up to the playground to greet their friends and start another day at Stormy Cliff School.

Chapter 2

Stormy Cliff School

There were sixteen children in the one class of Stormy Cliff School, all from the village and aged between nine and twelve – older pupils went to school on a neighbouring island. The classroom was quite small and they sat at old, wooden desks in rows, as instructed by the head teacher, Mr Traiton.

When the children entered the classroom in the mornings just before lessons started there was always quite a racket, with everyone trying to compete with the noise of the building shaking and creaking. It was tradition for them to do so, no matter what the weather.

Ben and Harriet would catch up with their best friends, William and Catherine, with whom they had formed the group 'The Crusaders' and would run around at break time pretending to be various characters from history, saving each other from perilous situations. Other members of the class, like Jack and Kieran, who were the oldest and tallest of them all, would talk loudly about the latest football scores of various teams, and some, like Jimmy, the youngest child who was small in size but big in imagination, chatted quietly about his supposed latest adventure. Finally, their class teacher, Mr Harris, would always rush in saying, 'Quiet children, you don't want to annoy the head teacher!'

Today the building seemed to be in a state of nervous tension and with the winds coming and going it kept violently shaking. In fact the noise was so loud that when Mr Harris entered and said his piece not one of the children heard him. Catherine was busy telling Ben and Harriet about her latest fishing trip in between rattles coming from the roof, with William chipping in occasionally, asking how their parents were – he always acted like he was grown up, which amused the others greatly. They only noticed that Mr Harris was there when he got to the front of the classroom.

Mr Harris was a very genuine, kind-hearted person. He was young as teachers go and cared very much for his position, understanding the importance of what he did and taking enjoyment from educating and inspiring his young students. Inspiration, however, was hard to find at the moment with the school in such difficult waters. According to Mr Traiton there wasn't a penny going spare, so Mr Harris couldn't buy art materials to do anything creative with the children and there was only a small selection of books to teach from, most of them out of date. Still, he tried his best and the children knew this and respected him for it.

As they all settled down into their seats, Ben and Harriet moving into the second row next to William and Catherine, Mr Harris started the lesson.

'I hope you all had a good weekend. Did anyone get up to anything fun?' He always tried to begin as positively as possible. The children were all sitting politely and paying attention.

'I went fishing!' said Catherine keenly, as if it were a new experience for her.

'Oh, and did you have any more success than last time?' asked Mr Harris brightly.

'Not really. I still didn't catch anything, not even an old boot.' She had failed to mention this to Ben and Harriet and after the way she had been talking about it before they were rather disappointed.

'Oh well, keep trying – you never know when a fish will pop up and say hello. How about someone else? Did anyone do anything they've never done before, or even better something you've always dreamed of?' As Mr Harris said this, Jimmy, who was sitting in the front row and always eager to impress, perked up.

'I flew to the moon in a big red space rocket!' he stated proudly.

'Did you really?' asked Mr Harris.

'No he didn't,' said Jack from the back, rolling his eyes.

'Well I dreamt about it anyway,' said Jimmy, a little dejectedly.

'And who says dreams can't come true,' said Mr Harris, lifting Jimmy's spirits again. 'I've always dreamed of finding a big pot of treasure in my garden, and I'm sure that one day I will.' He looked upwards in reflection and was greeted by a loud shake. 'Our roof really is making an awful racket today. How about you, Ben, Harriet, what did you do? How's your dad?' Ben and Harriet were two of Mr Harris's best students – hard workers and always willing to help. They had both their mother and father to thank for these qualities.

'Dad's ok,' Ben answered. 'He's just got to rest now. We helped Mum fix the fence by our pond.'

'It was hard work!' chipped in Harriet brightly.

'I bet you've got lots of muscles now,' joked Mr Harris.

'I hope not!' Harriet quickly replied, making her teacher smile.

'Anyway, we must crack on,' he said, moving on to his planned lesson. 'We could have a lot to get through. I thought we could continue looking at the history of Thistlewick and then start drawing maps of the island. I had a hunt around but I still couldn't find any more text books, so I'm afraid I will have to read to you, then I'll pass the one book I do have around so that you can draw your maps from it.'

'I don't have a pencil, Mr Harris,' said Jack.

'Well you can borrow mine, Jack.' Mr Harris walked over to his desk and took a solitary pencil out of the pot on top of it, which he gave to Jimmy to pass backwards.

'Thank you,' said Jack.

'Not at all.'

Mr Harris bent down to one of the drawers in his desk and with some effort pulled a severely aged book out, lifting it up carefully and turning to the page he had marked with a note.

'This book does appear to be about fifty years out of date, so it may not be totally accurate any more,' he said. Moving to the front of his desk and propping himself up against it, he began to read. 'The island of Thistlewick is so named after its discoverer, Lord Samuel Lewis Thistlewick, who found the island in 1712 when he was marooned off its coast. The island has an array of interesting features including many crevices and coves to explore, a mysterious forest and, despite the treacherous waters surrounding it, a thriving fishing fleet. A local warlock has predicted that the first mission to the moon will take off from Thistlewick in ten years' time.' He paused after saying this; Jimmy put his hand up abruptly.

'But sir, hasn't the first mission to the moon already happened in America?'

'Yes it has Jimmy, well done. As I said, this book is out of date. We'll forget that bit I think; do point out anything else that's incorrect as I read,' he said to the class in general, looking back down to the book. 'In 1903, a consortium of ramblers...'

Mr Harris was cut off mid sentence by the sound of the door opening at the end of the classroom. As he looked up and the whole class turned around, they saw the looming figure of their head teacher in the half shadow. Some of them jumped and others froze in their seats. Mr Traiton was a tall, imposing man, dressed in an expensive looking suit, and as he stepped into the classroom, darkness seemed to follow him in. From the back of the room he spoke loudly to Mr Harris, his voice booming.

'Ah, Harris, I hope you're using that textbook well, it cost me money you know!'

'Well, it's a bit of a struggle really, sir,' Mr Harris replied, a weakness suddenly showing in his voice. 'We could do with a few more, to tell the truth.'

'Rubbish! You've always managed before with just the one. I mean, can the children even read?' He glared around the classroom. Some of the children stared at him and others avoided eye contact.

'Yes we can, sir!' said Jack indignantly.

'I'll believe that when I see it,' the head teacher retorted, passing the comment off. 'Now, Harris, I'm here because I want you to send two of your children to my office right this instant. I have an important job for them.'

'Oh, and what's that?' Mr Harris asked with nervous suspicion – the head teacher didn't usually want to see the children anywhere, let alone in his office.

'A private matter, you'll find out soon.'

'Well, we are in the middle of a lesson. Can it wait until afterwards?'

'Certainly not! I need them now. This is more important than any lesson you may be teaching.' Mr Traiton seemed to rise up as he spoke and his voice became louder and more threatening.

'Right then.' Mr Harris glanced cautiously around the room, thinking of who would be brave enough to encounter the head teacher alone. His eyes came to the twins. 'Ben and Harriet, could you go with Mr Traiton, please?'

'Ah, brother and sister, perfect. Come with me.' Mr Traiton signalled to Ben and Harriet and walked out through the door.

The two children both turned to their class teacher, looking and feeling apprehensive; he looked apologetically back. They didn't say anything and instead rose up from their chairs, picking up their bags as they left.

'Good luck,' said Mr Harris quietly as they walked out of the room. He wondered what the head teacher had planned for them.

Chapter 3

Mr Traiton's Mission

The heavy oak door of Mr Traiton's office stood high in front of the twins; they had never been allowed near here before and were quite intimidated. The head teacher pushed the door open and they walked slowly in after him. As they crossed the threshold their eyes met a very gothic and overly imposing room, its harsh tube lighting contrasting with the dark wooden surroundings. Two of the walls were hidden behind rows of shelves and cupboards, which were full of worn trophies and faded certificates – possibly all of the school's achievements from its two hundred year existence locked away in this one room. There was only one small window and a large desk at the centre of the office. The impression Ben and Harriet had got from the door was only heightened by what they saw inside it; even Ben felt right to be scared, although he did think the room suited Mr Traiton well.

Behind the desk stood Mr Foxsworth, the head teacher's repressed, rodent-like dogsbody. 'Silent but deadly,' the children all said when they saw him scuttling around the school like a rat being chased by a large cat, looking after Mr Traiton's every need. Maybe he was a good person working in the wrong job, they didn't know – he certainly didn't seem very comfortable. Now, though, he spoke quickly and eagerly, as if trying to impress his master.

'I found another new machine, Mr Traiton, sir. We could buy it from Wielding if…'

'Quiet, Foxsworth!' Mr Traiton cut him off abruptly, lowering his voice to say, 'the children will hear.' Turning back to the children his voice became booming once more. 'Move in, children, move in.'

He gestured at Ben and Harriet to move to the front of his desk and then proceeded to sit down behind it in a large chair worthy of a devilish king. Foxsworth moved to the back of the room and assumed a position resembling a hamster frozen in fright. The children stood uncomfortably, waiting for Mr Traiton to tell them what he wanted.

'Now,' he said. 'You may have noticed that Stormy Cliff is in a spot of bother.'

'How do you mean, sir?' asked Ben.

'I know you aren't receiving the education you deserve and, frankly, this building is falling apart,' replied Mr Traiton matter-of-factly. 'I would *love* to help you more, but we're rather short on cash you see, especially with those heavy teacher wages and the er... the giant... erm...'

'Bees,' Foxsworth chipped in quickly.

'Yes bees. The bees that ruined my office. Had to smoke the blighters out and purchase new furniture.'

Ben and Harriet looked at each other with raised eyebrows – that was a bit far fetched.

'It was a big job,' Foxsworth said from his position behind the head teacher.

'Would you be quiet, Foxsworth!' Mr Traiton fired at his dogsbody. 'In short, the school is running out of money, and I'll be honest with you children, we need it desperately, or Stormy Cliff will be closed down.'

'Closed! Oh no!' Ben and Harriet both said in shock. They suddenly found their hearts plummeting to their stomachs. What would they do without Stormy Cliff? They'd have to go to boarding school on another island and move away from their friends and family. They didn't want that.

'Fortunately, I have a plan to save Stormy Cliff School,' said Mr Traiton after a calculated pause.

'A very cunning plan,' Foxsworth attempted to join in again. This time he was merely treated with a stern glare from the head teacher, and he moved over to a corner of the room and gazed into a cabinet. The children's hearts lifted a little bit.

'Now listen carefully,' Mr Traiton continued. 'There have been a lot of shipwrecks off Thistlewick Island, and many of these ships carried cargoes of gold. There is one wreck in particular whose treasure has never been accounted for, and I think I have a plan for you to find it.'

'Us, sir? Treasure? Are you asking Ben and me to go on a treasure hunt?' Harriet spoke up for the first time, intrigued by what the head teacher was saying, if not a little taken aback.

'Yes, dear girl. I have chosen the both of you to find this treasure and with it help me save the school. I would retrieve it myself, of course, but I am far too old to be an adventurer, and the school couldn't cope without me. So I want you two, brother and sister, to be ambassadors for Stormy Cliff. You will find the money that will save it.'

There was a long pause after this statement; the children were left speechless – this was big.

'Come on, you're children, you're meant to get excited about this sort of thing.'

'Well, it does sound awfully exciting,' said Ben cautiously. 'But are we going to be safe doing that?'

'Of course. What harm could come to two young children like you going to find some treasure. You only have to locate it, pick it up and bring it back to me.'

'Mr Harris would be so proud of us, and we can make Stormy Cliff a better place for us all!' Harriet felt a surge of importance run up her spine.

'Indeed. So you'll do it then?' Mr Traiton asked eagerly.

'Yes, if it will help,' said Ben.

'Oh yes, it will help me… I mean us, tremendously.'

'Will you tell our parents about this, sir?' Harriet asked.

'Of course. I'll ring them later and tell them exactly what their special children are doing for me.'

'Ok, thank you.' It sounded perfectly fine to Ben so far.

'Right, your instructions then. Make sure you remember them. I don't have the foggiest what the ship you must find is called or where it is – I only heard about it the other day. The fishermen down by the harbour will know where the shipwreck is located – they know about all the ships, past and present, so you must go and see them.'

'Right,' said Ben as Harriet got a notebook out of her bag to write the instructions down.

'But first you need the name of the ship. If you visit the church, the vicar holds the island's records, so he should be able to tell you. You must ask him for the name of the ship whose treasure is unaccounted for.'

'Ok, well that doesn't sound too bad,' said Ben, although he had a feeling it would probably be harder than Mr Traiton was letting on.

'So, first to the church, then to the harbour to see the fishermen. After that you are on your own and must find the treasure. When you have it, you must bring it straight back to me. Understood? It is vital that you succeed, or Stormy Cliff will be no more.'

'We won't fail you, sir!' said Ben.

Harriet, on the other hand, stayed quiet. She was beginning to realise the enormity of what they would have to do – so much of it was unknown.

'Oh, and children,' the head teacher said as they began to move towards the door. 'There are always some pretty silly rumours going around about the ships that were wrecked off Thistlewick. If anyone mentions anything about supernatural goings on – ghosts or anything like that – just ignore them.'

'Ok,' said Ben, almost at the door.

'Off you go then.' And with this, Mr Traiton saw them out of his office.

CHAPTER 4

The Journey Begins

'Do you think we should go home and tell Dad before we go too far?' Harriet asked. The twins had walked out of the school gate and down onto the village green, ready to start their adventure, but Harriet was still feeling a bit uncertain.

'Mr Traiton's going to tell him, remember?' said Ben. He sat down casually on a bench at the edge of the green, placing his school bag on the ground beside him. Harriet followed suit, sitting upright with her hands in her lap.

'But still, I'm not sure,' she said slowly.

'It'll be fine. We're not going to be that long. I mean how big can this island be?'

'We don't know, we've never been north of the village.'

'Well, we don't even know where the treasure is yet,' Ben persisted. 'It might be hidden somewhere on the south of the island.' It was in this sort of situation, when confidence and courage were needed in the face of the unknown, that Ben usually became the positive party and Harriet the doubting one. 'I think we should find out where it is first and then decide what to do.'

'Ok,' Harriet said, still unsure about it all.

Sitting up, Ben looked at his sister in a very brotherly way, understanding how she was feeling. 'You're nervous, aren't you?'

'No, not really. Well, maybe a little. I'm glad Mr Harris chose us, but Mr Traiton scares me.'

'He is a bit of a creep, isn't he? And that office really was scary. But think about it, we came to school today prepared to face another boring day and now we're setting out on an adventure together. Imagine Will and Catherine and all the others sitting there in the classroom, bored stiff, while we're out here on a treasure hunt! A school day can't get much more exciting than this!'

'Yes, I suppose so.' Harriet sighed and slowly a smile appeared on her face. 'What are we waiting for then, let's get to the church.' She stood up and waited for Ben before walking off.

'We haven't been there for a long time, not since last Christmas with Dad,' he said as they moved over the green. 'Those were good times, weren't they?'

CHAPTER 5

The Book of Records

'That's a fantastic collection of flowers you've got there, Miss Susan, I can smell them from here,' the vicar said to his assistant and flower arranger across the church, before picking up a large pile of hymn books.

'Why, thank you Vicar, they're nearly finished. I'll be done soon.' Miss Susan's strong Irish accent added character to her words. She had been bought up in the gardens of a nunnery in Southern Ireland and moved to Thistlewick as a teenager, so was perfectly equipped to deal with flower arranging in the village church.

Set in idyllic land and surrounded by a neat square of tall trees, Thistlewick church was a large building. The heart of the community, it was divided into sections – the main church, the village hall and the meeting room for the village council. The vicar, Thomas Fareway, had grown up on the island and knew a lot about its history, having kept its records since he was ten. Now thirty, he was fairly new to the church, having been the vicar for only three years. In the island's tradition he was quickly accepted as the head of the church and now everyone simply called him Vicar. With the help of Miss Susan he had turned the church into a fun and vibrant place to visit. There were regular activity days and craft shops, encouraging children and adults alike to be creative. Today, the vicar and Miss Susan were preparing for the wedding of a young couple who had just moved to Thistlewick.

The vicar watched Miss Susan potter about, placing plants in colourful arrangements around the church while he distributed the hymn books among the pews. After a while he spoke tentatively.

'Miss Susan, when you've finished, would you care to join me for afternoon tea at the vicarage?'

Miss Susan stopped arranging a particularly large collection of chrysanthemums and stood up, smiling sweetly between flowers. 'Why, Vicar, if you insist, I've just baked a cake, so I can bring that over. It's a new recipe I've been working on.'

'Well, that sounds fantastic. I always love your cakes – you should be working as a top class cake maker rather than arranging flowers here for me.'

'You do flatter me sometimes, Thomas!' Her face started to turn as red as the roses next to her. 'But I do love working here with you.'

As they smiled at each other, there was a fumbling at the big church door and they both jumped in surprise, several hymn books falling from the vicar's hands. Through the door came Ben and Harriet.

'Oh, hello children,' the vicar said, flustered. 'You gave us a bit of a scare there. That door does loom over the church somewhat.'

'It's rather difficult to open too,' said Harriet, her and Ben having had to push against the door with their backs to open it. When they entered it had almost seemed like the vicar and Miss Susan were flirting with each other.

'Well, anyway, what a pleasant surprise,' the vicar continued, picking up the dropped hymn books and placing them on a pew. 'We don't see you here much these days, ever since the fête for Save the Whales. You did well then.'

The children remembered that event well. They had run a successful attraction, charging people to throw wet sponges at their dad's head. Mrs Davies won with the most hits and she had never let her husband forget it. That was last year.

'Our dad's still ill so we haven't been able to get out much,' said Ben.

'And Mum's really busy at the moment,' added Harriet.

'Well, send them my best wishes. I hope you'll all be able to come along to help me decorate the tree at Christmas, that's always a happy time. Anyway, it's nice to see you here now. What can I do for you?'

Harriet stood tall, feeling important. 'We're here on business. School business.'

'Oh right,' chuckled the vicar. 'Did Mr Harris send you?'

'No, our head teacher, Mr Traiton,' said Ben.

'I see.' The vicar's expression changed, becoming slightly wary.

'We need to know the name of a ship. One that was wrecked off Thistlewick,' Ben continued.

'Well, there have been more shipwrecks off the shores of Thistlewick than there are bodies buried in my churchyard, although a fair few of those bodies have come from the ships, mind. But all the shipwrecks we have recorded will be in my Book of Records for the island.'

'So you'll be able to find it then?' Harriet asked.

'The records are quite extensive, I can assure you; it'll be in there somewhere. Miss Susan, could you pop into the vestry and get my Book of Records please.'

'Which one's that, Vicar?' Miss Susan asked over a collection of sweet peas she was busy positioning around the choir pews.

'It's the biggest one on the bookshelf in the corner, you can't miss it.'

'Right you are.' She wandered off through a curtain at the front of the church.

'Sit down, sit down,' the vicar gestured keenly to Ben Harriet, directing them to a pew. He sat in the one opposite them, placing the hymn books in front of him. 'So why do you want the name of this ship then? Is it a school project?'

'I suppose you could put it that way,' replied Ben. 'We've been sent to find some treasure.'

'Treasure, ay, and how does that relate to school?'

'Mr Traiton needs the money to save Stormy Cliff. We have to get it otherwise the school will be closed,' Harriet emphasised.

'Well, I knew there were problems but I didn't realise Stormy Cliff was quite that desperate. I would offer up some of the church funds, but we're pretty tight on money ourselves at present.'

Miss Susan came staggering back in carrying an incredibly large book, almost half her size in height.

'Well I never, Miss Susan, the children are on a hunt to find treasure, it's what you'd read in a book,' the vicar said to her as she placed the Book of Records on the pew in front of him.

'It's not something you hear about every day, certainly,' she panted, out of breath.

They all turned their attention to the Book of Records. The gold writing, placed against a red front cover, stated that it contained 'The Records of Thistlewick Island'. The vicar winced slightly as he carefully picked it up, opened it and started flicking through the thin pages. It was apparent to the children that a great deal of care had been taken over keeping the book in good condition. The vicar stopped at a page that had the title 'Fatality at Sea', with an index underneath it.

'Right, shipwrecks, page 1100,' he said, referencing the index. 'So this is a ship which carried treasure?'

'Yes, and the treasure hasn't been found,' replied Ben.

'So it is lost, unaccounted for? Well that will narrow it down for us then. There are hundreds of ships and a lot of them had treasure, but I think in most cases it has been accounted for over time. Let me see. Ok, here we are… shipwrecks.' The vicar had reached a page with a large table covering it, the rows and columns crowded with small printed information. 'It's lucky my eyesight is still as good as it is. I'll look in the treasure column for "unaccounted".' He ran his finger down the column, scanning each entry meticulously, until after a long while he came to what he was looking for.

'Found anything?' Ben asked hopefully.

'Yes, it looks like there are three ships that are under the category of "unaccounted". Now we just need to narrow them down. Let's see, the most recent is a ship called "Gertrude", with a Captain Penny. An unknown vessel that crashed and sank in 1933.'

'What an odd name for a ship,' said Harriet.

'Yes, well most ships in those days had female names. Maybe Gertrude was a particularly popular one,' the vicar pondered. 'Now, I think I remember one of the fishermen telling me a story about that ship. Ah yes, that was it – his father was fishing one day and caught some gold in his net. When he dived down to take a look he found the ship and all its gold. I'm told it turned out to be fool's gold, though; he was rather disappointed. Right, I need to alter that record then, seeing as it's incorrect.'

He took out a pencil and made the adjustment, fixing it to say 'found and disqualified' under the treasure column.

'The second ship, from 1902, is called "Titan", a rather impressive name, captain unknown, and type of ship is merchant. Now, the story behind this one is that it ran into trouble about a mile off Thistlewick, sank, and the remains became buried in the sand close to the west of the island. There was an official dive for it by the local Sub Aqua Club – they found nothing of any value and think that anything of great prosperity would have been thrown overboard somewhere in the middle of the ocean. So I don't think your ship will be that one.'

'There's only one left then, so it must be this next one,' Ben said, feeling a rush of excitement that was shared by Harriet.

'Well, let's have a read.' The vicar returned to the book. 'This ship is called "Tormenta", with a captain by the name of Roger Traiton and a crew size of approximately twenty. The type of ship is pirate.'

'Pirate!' Ben and Harriet exclaimed in unison.

'I hope we don't bump into any pirates!' said Harriet, her body tense.

'Don't worry, Harriet, they'll be long dead by now,' the vicar said, reassuring her. 'Now this one seems like what you're looking for. The treasure is unaccounted for and apparently the ship crashed just off the north of Thistlewick in a storm and sank nearby. It is rumoured that the treasure is hidden somewhere inland.'

'That has to be it then,' said Ben confidently.

'I'm afraid I have no information other than that. I suggest you go and see the fishermen – if anyone does, they will know of the ship's location, and they might be able to tell you a tale or two about it.'

'Ok, that's what Mr Traiton said we'd have to do,' said Ben.

'Hang on… Traiton. Did you say the captain of the Tormenta was called Roger Traiton?' asked Harriet.

'Yes, that's right, Roger Traiton,' replied the vicar.

'Do you think that's a coincidence?' she said.

'I wouldn't be surprised if it was more than a coincidence, if it was your head teacher who told you about the ship in the first place.'

'Mr Traiton's a creep,' said Ben. 'I wouldn't be surprised if he came from a long line of pirates!'

'I'm sure he is a good person really. He does, after all, want to use this treasure to save your school.'

'That's true. Right, we'd better go and see the fishermen.' Ben stood up and moved to shake the vicar's hand. 'Thank you very much.'

'My pleasure. Now you two be careful. I know you've got sensible heads on you but I don't want to have to deal with your funerals in my time as vicar.'

'Don't say that! You'll scare me,' said Harriet, nervously.

'I'll try to control her,' said Ben, cheekily.

'Oi!' his sister said.

'Joking apart, no dangerous climbing or swimming or anything that will get you into trouble,' warned the vicar.

'We promise. Thank you for your help.'

'Bye then.' The vicar looked after them as they walked out of the church doors and into the now overcast day, putting their coats on as they went.

As the doors closed behind them, the children paused only briefly to gaze up into a solid grey sky and then skipped down the path on their way to see the fishermen.

Chapter 6

Cunning Mr Traiton

'Right. Davies,' said Mr Traiton to no one in particular as he filed through the school contacts.

He picked up the phone receiver from his desk and dialled the number of the Davies household, sitting back in his chair as it began to ring. Foxsworth was, as always, standing in the background like a statue conveying a nervous disposition. The phone rang a few times and at the other end of the line, Mr Davies sat up in bed and stretched over to pick up the receiver from his bedside table.

'Hello, Stan Davies here.'

'Hello Mr Davies, this is Tristan Traiton, head teacher at Stormy Cliff. I'm just ringing to tell you about your children, Ben and Harriet.'

'Right, are they ok?'

'Well, it depends on how you look at it. They're in a spot of trouble you see.'

'They aren't in any danger, are they?'

'No, no, nothing like that. I'm afraid your children haven't been behaving as we would have liked them to. There was an incident with stealing and their teacher, Mr Harris, has become concerned over time about their disruptiveness.'

'What?!' Mr Davies exclaimed. 'But Ben and Harriet are good children, they've never been in trouble before. I don't understand. How long has this been happening?'

'It has been going on for some time. We didn't tell you because we didn't want you to worry.' The head teacher maintained a level voice, but gave enough expression to make what he was saying sound effective. 'However, when poor young Jimmy burst into my office in floods of tears, I'm afraid I had to move to the final measure.'

'The final measure! What are you talking about?' Mr Davies felt his blood pressure rising as he started to panic.

'We're sending your children to a boarding school on the mainland. They will only be there for a short while, but it should fix the problems that they have been having.'

Mr Davies really could not believe what he was hearing. 'Hold on,' he said, trying to compose himself. 'Let me call my wife and explain all this to her. She won't be able to get to you until after school hours, but she'll be down as soon as she can and you can talk it through with her and the children then. There must be another solution.'

'I'm afraid Ben and Harriet have already been taken away. They'll be half way across the sea by now.'

'What?! You can't do this, Traiton, it has to be illegal. It isn't fair on the children or us!'

'The law sets out that I should handle the case like I have. I am merely following procedure.'

'Well, I don't know what to say. My wife will be down later and you can answer to her then.' Mr Davies was shocked – disgusted – but more than anything concerned for his children.

'Ok, that's fine by me. Goodbye Mr…' But Mr Traiton was cut off as Mr Davies put down the phone. The head teacher slowly replaced the receiver at his end, his face contorting into a cruel grin.

CHAPTER 7

The Fishermen's Tale

'Ted!' shouted Albert Gailsborough, calling excitedly to his fellow fisherman over the wind, which was picking up again and rattling around the boats, causing them to bob up and down as if fighting against an invisible force. As Ted, a sturdily built but kind-hearted man of the sea, strolled over, Albert continued. 'Look what I caught in the puddle off yonder yesterday, isn't it massive?' He held out a rather fat cod – a fish abundantly caught off the island in the winter season – a bit too eagerly, almost throwing it at Ted.

'Well, that is a corker, Albie, but what have I told you, you can't catch cod, or any other fish for that matter, in puddles,' Ted said, both his bushy eyebrows raised. Albert was the oldest of the fishermen and it seemed to the other two that he was becoming more deluded by the day – they were used to this sort of conversation.

'You can! My mate Bernie caught fifty carp in a headwind on a puddle once,' Albert argued, his voice still eager.

'Oh aye, and where was that then?'

'It's the one just in front of… oh, what's the place… America!'

'Ah, you mean the Atlantic?'

'Yeah, the Atlantic puddle. That's the one,' Albert said confidently, still waving the fish around.

'That's not a puddle, you lobster net,' Ted chuckled. 'That's an ocean.'

'Oh.' Albert lowered his fish slowly. 'You mean after sixty years out there in a boat, I never knew that?'

'I'm sure you did once, Albie. But these days, with the wind and the spray, you're going a bit mad, my friend.' Ted spoke affectionately. No matter how mad old Albert was, he was still one of the team and a great storyteller, even if his stories sometimes bore no relation to reality. 'You go put that fish in the barrel with the rest of 'em.'

'The sea taught me everything I know. Perhaps one day it'll teach you a thing or two,' Albert muttered as he hobbled past Ted with the fish limp in his hand, towards the big barrel in which all the cod were stored before being distributed across the island.

As Ted moved over to his boat to untangle the rigging there was a big gust of wind and it began to gently rain.

'It's days like these that remind me why I enjoy being a fisherman,' said Ernie, the third member and head of the fishing fleet, as he came out of their small, wooden hut. 'I can't wait to get out there later and feel the spray against my face.'

Ernie was middle-aged and tall, wearing a heavy over-coat over a slender body. Everything about him, from the windswept hair to the strong smell of fish, revealed his love for his livelihood – in fact all three fishermen were like this. The harbour they inhabited was tiny, with only a few traditional fishing boats tied up, the rickety hut and a small collection of barrels and nets, now reasonably full with fish, placed on a raised platform above the tide. It didn't need to be any bigger than this though – the harbour was all the island needed for its supply of fish.

As Ernie began to sort through the fish in one of the barrels, he spotted two small figures on the path above the beach; they grew bigger and moved down the path and onto the beach beside the harbour. Even though they were wrapped up well in their coats, he knew these children well.

'Ben, Harriet, how nice to see you!' he said, heartily. The children's father had sometimes helped the fishermen out at weekends – before he fell ill, of course – so they knew the fishermen well. They stopped the other side of Ernie's barrel and he put the small, lifeless cod he was holding down before continuing. 'You can tell your dad he can come back

37

whenever he's ready; I know he enjoyed giving us a hand, and we appreciate the help.'

'Will do,' Ben smiled.

Ted walked over to join them, now finished with his boat. 'And you can tell your mum how much I enjoyed her cake at the village meeting the other day. It was marvellous.'

The four of them smiled.

'So what brings you all the way down here on a school day?' asked Ernie.

'We've been sent here on a mission by our head teacher, Mr Traiton,' informed Harriet, a certain pride in her words.

'Oh aye. You're not looking for work experience, are you?' asked Ted.

'No, not really,' said Ben.

'You'd make a fine fisherman, lad; it's the best job in the world. All you need to know is what fish to look for and where the oceans are on a map,' Ernie enthused.

'And you need a good spirit, mind!' chipped in Ted. 'Isn't that right, Albie?' But Albert didn't respond – he was off in his own world, staring out to sea.

'Well, I'm not really sure yet.' Ben didn't really want to be a fisherman but he also didn't want to offend them.

'Ah, I'm sure you'll get there one day. And Harriet, you'll take after your mum, I suppose; I bet culinary skills as good as hers run in the family. That cake really was a lov…'

But Ted was cut off by a sudden loud clap of thunder that made everyone jump, including a seagull staring longingly at the barrel of fish in front of it. It fell off the net it was standing on and, giving a begrudging squawk, flew over to a tree. With decidedly wintry intentions, the heavens quickly opened and it started to pour down with cold rain. Harriet pulled her hood up tightly around her face.

'C'mon, let's make a run for it. Everyone into the hut.' Ernie pulled his overcoat over his head too, and made a hobbled dash towards the hut. Ben and Harriet followed, the door rapidly swinging open for them.

'Albie, we're going inside.' Ted walked over to the old boater and patted him on the shoulder. He was still gazing out to sea with a puzzled look. 'Albie?'

'Going inside? With the kids?' Albert asked, vaguely, his mind still sailing around in his own thoughts.

'Yep. Why don't you come and tell them a story or two?'

At this Albert perked up. 'Stories, now I got a fair few of them I could tell!'

They both walked over to the hut and shut the door quickly behind them. As they did, a surprising amount of the sound caused by the rain and wind was shut out. The fishermen sat down on stools to one side of the hut, Albert on his traditional storytelling stool. Harriet pulled her hood down and joined Ben in sitting down on a bench opposite them. The hut was tiny and they were packed tightly together; the walls were lined with tackle and various bits and pieces that Ben assumed had something to do with fishing, as he stared around.

'It's not much, but it's a good place to come in weather like this,' Ted said, noticing Ben's wandering eyes. 'We sit here and reminisce about the old times.'

'My speciality.' Albert grinned at the children. He had a lovely, wrinkly face – Harriet thought – full of character.

As the rain continued to pour down outside, it suddenly seemed to get very dark. Ernie leant over to turn the light on; he pulled the chord and the hut soon found a friendly feel and a warm glow, the light bulb swinging around erratically.

'So, you said you were on a mission, didn't you?' Ted continued.

'Yes,' said Harriet. 'We're in search of a ship called Tormenta. It was wrecked…'

'Tormenta!' Albert cut her off in surprise, his eyes widening and his mouth opening uncharacteristically quickly. 'I haven't heard mention of that ship for many a year.'

'No, I'd almost forgotten about that one too,' agreed Ernie, equally as taken aback. 'By heck, that's one of the most… the most…'

'Famously feared pirate ships to roam our shores,' Ted finished the sentence gravely. 'And it crashed just off Thistlewick too, its crew swept away and its treasures rumoured to have been lost when it sank.'

'So you know about it then?' asked Ben.

'Boy, I can tell you the story of the Tormenta better than any man on this island,' Albert said, his blue eyes brightening, not quite with the excitement they had shown over his fish, but with more of an awe visible in them. He leant forwards towards the children. 'Nowadays it's a forgotten ship, irrelevant in today's world – only us fishermen really know about it. But back in my grandfather's day, when it crashed, it was the biggest news they had ever heard. You listen closely, children, and I'll tell you the tale of how the Tormenta came to an end.'

'We're listening!' exclaimed Harriet and Ben, almost together in eagerness. Now was their chance to unravel some of the mystery they found themselves a part of.

'It were back in 1880, when my grandfather had just joined the fishing fleet. He was eighteen. Back then Thistlewick was a quiet but thriving fishing paradise, much greater than it is today. No one off the island really knew about it, but the islanders were happy about that.'

Albert's voice rolled lyrically around every word as he started to tell his story with a passion, meaning Ben and Harriet had to concentrate hard to understand what was being described to them.

'One night there was a great storm, the worst they had seen for years. The winds tore through the whole island and the rough sea hit further inland than my grandfather had seen before, nearly ripping the fishing hut in half, it was that powerful. It was on this dark and fateful night that the Tormenta crashed. Earlier that day, before sunset, my grandfather's best friend, Alfie had sailed round to the north of the island and set up his telescope on top of Watcher's Cliff. I don't know why he was there – perhaps it was for stargazing – but as he looked through the telescope he saw a great ship heading towards him, about half a mile away and lit powerfully by its own lights. A pirate ship if ever there was one. Now, in those days there was no way of calling back to the south of the island to let them know about it, and there was no way he was going to venture back in his boat with the sea like it was and a pirate ship so near by. So he just had to stand there and watch as the devilish ship came nearer and nearer. As it did, a thick mist began to form around it, almost warning him of the ship's evil. It grew closer to the island and through the mist he was just able to make out a name written on its side.'

'Tormenta,' gasped Harriet, her eyes fixed on Albert, her mouth open.

'Aye, Tormenta,' replied Albert with a shake in his voice. 'And back then even the islanders on Thistlewick knew that name well and feared it. This ship was the most dangerous vessel around, so why was it heading towards Thistlewick, Alfie thought – there was nothing here for the pirates to take and he would have been surprised if they had even seen the blacked-out island. But as the ship got nearer and the waves crashed fiercely into it, there was a huge cracking sound, rumoured to have been heard even from the south of the island. The ship sank a hundred metres off Stowaway Cove. Soon after, Alfie heard the cries of the pirates swimming to shore. He ran away as fast as he could, leaving his telescope and boat behind him – pirates were coming to Thistlewick! But alas, no pirates were ever seen on the island, certainly not in the south, and it's thought that most of them, if not all, perished that night, captured by the sea.'

Albert sat back on his stool and let the effect of his tale settle in on the children. Ben and Harriet both continued to stare at him and then slowly turned to each other with mixed expressions of shock and wonderment. It was quite a story and they didn't know how to react. After a while Ben thought of a question.

'Have you ever investigated the shipwreck?' he asked, hoping for more details.

'No! None of us,' Albert said sharply.

Ben was puzzled by this reaction. 'But why? If you've known the location for so long, how come you've never gone to take a look?'

'Albert's only told you half the story,' said Ernie, deeply. 'It's rumoured that some of the pirates did live that night, and they dragged their treasure up the beach at Stowaway Cove and into a cave there, eventually dying with it. Many people have tried to uncover the ship and its treasure before our time, and those who came back told tales of the ghosts of those pirates haunting the entire cove, as well as the ship and the cave the treasure is meant to be hidden in. They are guarding over their treasure and will do so for all eternity, showing no sympathy for anyone who tries to take it. Ghosts are dangerous beings not to be reckoned with. That is why we and anyone else who remembers don't go near that cove and why the Tormenta has now been forgotten by most.'

Harriet looked slowly towards Ben again, a worried expression covering her face. Ben looked back at her, his expression unchanged. These sorts of stories always affected Harriet. Admittedly, Ben thought, it was a good story, but that was it, it was only a story.

'So that is what we know about the Tormenta,' said Ted. 'It's a ship still shrouded in mystery and one we haven't thought about for a long time. So why, may I ask, did you want to know about it?'

'It's for a school research project,' Ben replied quickly, before Harriet could speak – he didn't want to tell the fishermen the real reason for their wanting to know because he knew they would try to stop him and Harriet from going on their journey. The fishermen were lovely people, but their tales shouldn't be trusted.

Harriet continued to stare at her brother, still worried and puzzled by his answer.

'Actually, you couldn't draw us a map of the shipwreck's location, could you?' he continued, taking advantage of this opportunity. 'It would be good to stick into the project.'

'Of course,' replied Ted. 'Albie, you'd better draw this, you know it better than me.' He pulled some old, damp paper and a pen out of a drawer in the corner of the hut and passed it to Albert.

'Now, let me see,' said Albert, thinking as he traced the pen in thin air. Then he put pen to paper and quickly drew a line, which was obviously meant to represent an outline of Thistlewick, followed by a cross. 'Here's the island and that's where the ship is located, on the north side, just there.' He pointed to the cross. 'It may not be perfectly accurate, none of us knows the precise location.'

'Thank you,' said Ben, taking the paper from Albert. It wasn't exactly detailed, but it would do.

'Are you ok, lass?' Ernie asked Harriet. 'You look a bit pale.'

'I don't know,' she replied quietly. She had a very uncomfortable feeling about the situation Ben and her were in.

'It is quite a story, isn't it, but don't you worry, that's what's going to make your project so exciting, I'm sure.' Ernie leant forward and patted her on the shoulder; she smiled weakly at him.

The hut seemed to have become a lot lighter now that the fishermen had stopped telling the dark story, and bright light was seeping through the cracks in the door and around the hut.

'Right, come on then, sis, we'd better be heading off,' Ben said, keen to get moving.

He stood up, holding Harriet's hand so that she had to follow. Ted moved to the door and pushed it open for them. There wasn't a heavy wind any more, so it swung gently open, although with a loud creak.

'Look fellers, the weather's all but cleared up now. We have sunlight!' Ted exclaimed. 'Let's get going with the boats.'

They all gradually filtered outside.

'Thank you very much for your help,' Ben said, turning to the three fishermen as they moved over to their boats.

'Pleasure, my lad,' called Ted.

'Any time,' said Ernie.

'Bye.' Ben waved as he and Harriet walked back up to the path leading inland. Albert turned to wave back at them, a smile once more creasing his face.

Once the children were back onto the path heading inland, Harriet spoke. 'Why did you lie to them, Ben?'

'I had to, otherwise they'd have tried to stop us from going.'

'But should we be going to Stowaway Cove? I don't like this at all. It's a pirate ship with ghosts and if the fishermen haven't been there's no way we should go.' She breathed in heavily.

'There's nothing to worry about, Harriet. The ship used to have pirates on it, but they died many years ago. You can't have been that worried by what the fishermen said – you don't believe in ghosts.' His sister looked at him uncertainly. 'They don't exist,' he emphasised. 'That was just an old fishing tale; I'm sure only the fishermen really believe it. Anyway, remember what Mr Traiton said – we should ignore any stories about ghosts.'

'I suppose so.'

'Look, now we have the location of our ship and the treasure, we're one step closer to saving Stormy Cliff!'

'Yes, we are,' Harriet admitted. 'Well, if you're confident then so am I.'

'Are you sure? Because if you're not, then we won't go.'

'No, I'm sure. They were just stories. Stormy Cliff is real and needs our help.'

'Excellent,' Ben smiled. 'Before we go too far can we visit the market? Now the weather's better I'd quite like a strawberry boater.' He broke into a confident stride and Harriet had to skip to keep up with him.

CHAPTER 8

The Market

It was quite a walk to the market – Thistlewick may only have contained one village, but it was very spread out over the south of the island; however, the children had moved further north and in the direction they needed to go. Although the ground was still damp from the rain, a strong midday sun now shone brightly overhead, and by the time Ben and Harriet had reached the collection of blue and red striped stalls placed around the village square, they were in need of a drink.

The village square was surrounded by some of the oldest buildings on the island; almost Tudor in style, each one overhung the ground below it precariously. There were four entrances into the square, one from each corner, and the market stalls were placed around the edge. Thistlewick market was different to a lot of markets because it was like a shop to the islanders and therefore ran on most days of the week. There were a variety of stalls selling a range of products – fish sold by Ernie's wife, milk and other farm produce, fresh flowers from Miss Susan's garden, and everything else the islanders needed and wanted.

Ben and Harriet entered from the southwest corner of the square and headed across to 'Dottie's Drinks', which sold their favourite range of refreshments (and a Thistlewick special), the 'boater'. They had never been to the market during school time before and were surprised to see it so full, mainly with older islanders hovering around the jam and sewing stalls.

As they passed through the square, a few of the stall tenders smiled at them. Ben looked longingly at an electronic 'Blue Swordsman' knight on horseback as they approached 'Past Toys', the historic toys stall; he'd wanted this knight for a few months now and had been promised it for Christmas.

'Come on, Ben, we haven't got time to be distracted,' said Harriet, casting a forceful look at her brother. She was also looking forward to her Christmas present from 'Past Toys' and didn't want to look in case her castle had sold out. As they turned away from the stall they caught a whiff of a strange smell – something like cooked vegetables and raw onions.

'Care for some boiled carrots, children?' said a woman called Gladys in a hoarse voice.

She stood in front of Harriet and wasn't much taller then her. As a description, 'completely bonkers' didn't seem to do Gladys justice, the children thought; she was the nearest thing the island had to a gypsy and no-one really knew much about her – where she came from, what her surname was or why she was quite so mad. She had certainly been around since Ben and Harriet's parents were children and just seemed to turn up all over the place.

'Boiled carrots?' Harriet questioned, looking amusedly at the shrivelled, orange objects poking out from under Gladys's shawls.

'Yes, my dear. Very juicy and full of flavour. Only fifty pence, and that's what I call a bargain!'

'No thank you,' said Harriet, smiling politely at Gladys, who continued to stare back at her for a few seconds, her deep eyes flickering. Then the gypsy walked past the two children and called back to them.

'Maybe you'll prefer my cabbage – it's popular amongst young children like you. I'll look out for you tomorrow, when I'll have it by the bucketful.'

She tottered off. Ben and Harriet stared at each other in bemusement and both giggled. They walked over to the drinks stall.

'What do you want, sis?' Ben asked.

'I'll have my usual, please, a raspberry boater. How are you going to pay for it?'

'I'll use my lucky silver coin.'

'But Ben, you can't spend that, you take your lucky coin everywhere with you, and you're going to need it on our adventure more than you ever have done before.'

'By the end of today, I'm going to have a lot of coins to choose from to be my new lucky coin, and the one I pick will be a lot bigger and shinier than this one. Now, a raspberry boater for you and a strawberry boater for me.' He left Harriet to go and buy their drinks.

'Hello Harriet,' a familiar voice said from over her shoulder as she stood waiting for Ben.

'Oh, hello Mrs Evans,' said Harriet, turning around to face her friend William's Mum.

'It's a surprise to see you here. You can tell your mum her cake went down a treat the other day,' said Mrs Evans, as Ben walked over to them carrying two drinks.

'I will do.'

'And Ben's here with you too. So why are you two out of school at this time?'

'We're on a treasure hunt,' said Harriet for the second time today; the effect still hadn't worn off.

'What sort of treasure hunt?'

'We have to find a ship called the Tormenta,' said Ben, as he placed a straw in his drink.

'Oh, and do your parents know about this?'

'Yes, Mr Traiton should have rung Dad by now,' Ben answered.

'I see,' said Mrs Evans with a suspicious tone in her voice. 'Well, I must be off to the church to help Miss Susan with the flower arrangements for the wedding on Thursday. I've just picked up these beautiful lilies to add to the collection.' She held out the flowers for the children to inspect.

'They smell lovely,' commented Harriet, holding one of the flowers to her nose.

'Yes, well, I'll see you soon I hope.' Mrs Evans started to head off. 'Bye.'

'Bye bye,' said Harriet. Her brother handed her the frothy raspberry drink she had requested and they moved over to a seat carved out of a tree trunk in the middle of the square. 'Shall we check our map, Ben?'

'Yep.' Ben pulled the map that Albert had scribbled for them out of his trouser pocket and unfolded it. 'It isn't really much of a map, is it?'

They looked at the loose outline of the island, with one large cross placed at the top of it.

'Well, at least we know we have to head north anyway. We've never been past the edge of the forest before,' said Ben.

'Do you remember when we were younger and all of us used to play out there – you, me, Catherine, William, Jack and the others. We used to dare each other to climb a tree on the edge of the forest and you were the only one who ever did.'

'Yeah and it was pretty scary up there too. All I can remember seeing were shadows moving around underneath me, and then Jack gave a wolf howl, which really made me jump.'

'Jack didn't do a wolf howl, Ben,' his sister said seriously.

'What, you mean that was an actual…'

'William did the wolf howl,' she cut him off, grinning.

'Oh, well that's ok then. Anyway, we were a lot younger back then. It's only a forest, same as any other.'

He started to sip at his drink as Harriet stared down at the map again, trying to imagine what was ahead of them. As she began to wonder what the shipwreck would look like after all these years, her thoughts were interrupted by a loud voice, which carried around the market.

'Toy swords for sale! Get your toy swords here! Only five pounds.'

It was Mr Sharpe, who sold a variety of toys, including toy swords, bow and arrow sets and water guns. Unlike the rest of the market sellers, who stood behind their stalls all day, Mr Sharpe preferred to stride around the square with a selection of his products tied to his waist. He was very popular with the children of the village.

As Harriet looked up she saw Simon and Bertie Granger, two small children below school age, pestering their mother to give them money to buy swords. Eventually Mrs Granger gave in and they skipped joyfully over to Mr Sharpe and purchased two long wooden swords. With a friendly smile he waved them off and they started to fight each other around the market stalls, laughing loudly. They began to head rapidly towards the seat Ben and Harriet were sitting on and before Harriet had a chance to warn her brother, Bertie tumbled into him, causing him to spill his drink on the floor. Ben glared at the two children as they quickly ran back to their mother.

'Are you all right, lad?' asked Mr Sharpe, walking over to Ben. 'Let me buy you another drink.'

'No, it's ok thank you,' said Ben, picking up the now empty cup. 'I'd nearly finished anyway.'

'Ok. So where are you off to today?' Mr Sharpe was a tall man, but his face was too friendly to be imposing.

'We've got to get to the north of the island,' replied Ben.

'Ah, well you'll have to head through the dark forest to reach there. It's not a place I'd advise children to go, the forest, but if you absolutely must?'

'Yes, it's very important,' said Harriet, earnestly.

'Well then, do you know where you have to go?'

'It's over that way,' said Ben, pointing to the northeast corner of the square. '… I think,' he added, uncertainly.

'I tell you what, I know an entrance into the forest, so I'll help you on your way and take you there. I could do with a break anyway.'

'Thank you,' said Ben.

'That's quite all right,' said Mr Sharpe.

After waiting for Harriet to finish her drink and then returning the cups to the 'Dottie's Drinks' stall, the three of them set off out of the square, heading out of the northwest exit and moving up the path on their way to the dark forest.

CHAPTER 9

Concerned Classmates

Back at Stormy Cliff, Mr Harris and the children were making the most of the afternoon sun and spending the first lesson after lunch in a field outside the school. The field, belonging to The White Wing pub, had an excellent view of Stormy Cliff and the children were all busy drawing their impressions of the school. Mr Harris walked around them admiring the drawings and giving advice where he felt it was needed.

'You've got the perspective really well there, Jess,' he said, bending down to look at the work of Jessica, a small, endearing girl with hexagonal-shaped glasses. 'And the way you've drawn the stonework really adds texture. Don't forget to draw in windows.'

'No sir,' Jessica smiled.

'That's it, Jack, you're getting the hang of it now. Once you've finished the outline you can add in more detail.'

Jack nodded and Mr Harris moved over to Jimmy, who was the most creative member of the class.

'Now, Jimmy, that is very impressive.' Jimmy's image was bold but detailed and captured every aspect of the school incredibly well. It was also beginning to look colourful. 'I love the way you've rubbed in the grass, it really brings your image to life.'

'Thank you, sir,' said Jimmy, turning round to face his teacher. 'I was going to add in some mud for Stormy Cliff.'

'That sounds excellent.'

'Sir…' Jimmy added tentatively. 'Where have Ben and Harriet gone?'

A few of the children turned around to look at Mr Harris at the mention of their classmates.

'I'm not entirely sure, Jimmy, but I think Mr Traiton is giving them some private lessons.' Mr Harris didn't really know what had happened to Ben and Harriet and was beginning to worry, but he felt it best not to let the rest of the class know this.

'Maybe they're on an adventure,' Catherine suggested enthusiastically.

'If they are they never said anything to us,' said William.

'It's a nice thought, but I doubt they are, Catherine. It would be good if we could all go on an adventure,' said Mr Harris. Some of the class nodded wistfully.

'I hope they'll be back soon,' said Rebecca, William's younger sister, who was very fond of the twins. 'Harriet is meant to be coming round after school to help me plant my miniature garden, isn't she William?'

'Yeah,' her brother replied. Ben was also supposed to be going over to play in William's new tree house.

'Don't worry, I'm sure they'll be back soon,' said Mr Harris, although he wasn't certain of this. Perhaps he should go and ask Mr Traiton about the situation at the end of school. 'Now, let's get these drawings finished, and then in the last lesson we can create our own adventure stories.'

The children settled back down to their drawings, still curious about what had happened to Ben and Harriet.

CHAPTER 10

The Forest of Shadows

'Very dark, isn't it? Even in this sunlight you can't see that far in,' said Mr Sharpe, his eyes straining.

They were standing at the edge of the forest, the crowded branches of thick trees hanging over them.

It had taken a while to get here – they had stopped for lunch in a sheep field at Lower Farm, the only farm on the south of the island, where Ben and Harriet had explained their mission to Mr Sharpe, and they hadn't been able to pass through another field because of a warning about snakes, meaning they had to take a longer route around.

However, they now stood gazing into the forest, the children wondering what lay ahead.

'The Forest of Shadows, they used to call it,' Mr Sharpe informed them. 'I wouldn't be put off by that, though, it's harmless really, apart from the lions and tigers and bears.'

'You… you are joking, aren't you?'

'Of course I am, Harriet. There shouldn't be anything in there that will harm you. I can't see why the place has got such a bad reputation, really.'

In all honesty it didn't look that scary to Ben or Harriet, but they could hardly see anything as they peered in and it was the unknown factor they found unnerving. However, if Mr Sharpe said there was nothing to worry about, then they trusted his judgement.

'This is where I must leave you – I need to get back to the market in time for the after school rush.'

'Well, thank you very much for your help, Mr Sharpe,' said Ben.

'My pleasure. With a cause like yours I only wish I could help further. In fact I'd like you to take one of my swords.' Mr Sharpe pulled a wooden sword from his belt and handed it to Ben. The sword was very well crafted, Ben thought, and had neat wispy engravings along the edge. 'It's a replica of a Great Sword.'

'It certainly is,' said Ben, gripping the sword firmly and raising it above his head to get a feel for it.

'No, I mean that is what it's called, a Great Sword,' Mr Sharpe smiled. 'I give it to you just in case you do meet anything you'd prefer not to. Simply pointing that at most animals will scare them away, I have found.'

'Ok.' Ben tucked the sword into a side strap on his school bag.

'So, you see that little path there?' Mr Sharpe pointed to a small path in front of them, leading into the forest, which neither Ben or Harriet had spotted before as it was heavily overgrown with plant life. 'If you walk along it, you should end up parallel to a track. At some point if you move over to the track, you'll be able to follow that along to reach northern Thistlewick.'

'Right,' Harriet took note.

'If you have any problems or need a place to rest or sleep if it gets too late, I have a friend in the north of the island. He's a farmer by the name of Andrew Potts, and has a nice big farm called Half Acre just outside the forest, to the left of the track. Just tell him Richard Sharpe sent you.'

'Ok, left of the track, Half Acre, Mr Potts,' said Ben. 'I recognise his name.'

'He's Kieran's uncle, I think. Kieran is in our class at Stormy Cliff,' Harriet explained to Mr Sharpe.

'Oh, right. So are you all set and clear about where you need to go?' he asked.

'I think so,' said Harriet, now with an added air of confidence she didn't have earlier that day. Ben nodded his agreement.

'Excellent, then together you will endeavour to find the treasure. I wish you the best of luck and I'll keep an eye out for Stormy Cliff. Stay safe and if anything goes wrong, head straight to Half Acre Farm.'

'Thank you very much,' said Ben again.

'Thank you,' said Harriet, and Mr Sharpe smiled and walked away, back to the market to earn his living.

The two children moved forward and slipped carefully between the towering trees and overgrown shrubs and weeds, setting off along the small path into the Forest of Shadows.

* * *

Ben and Harriet were now deep inside the forest. It was just as dark as it had promised to be and only occasionally was the shadowy world broken by light filtering through the treetops. The trees were even more tightly packed together now, almost ganging up on the twins.

'We should have brought a torch,' whispered Ben. He didn't know why he spoke so quietly, but it just seemed the sort of place where you should.

Harriet didn't reply and simply squeezed his hand, continuing to hold it tightly as they walked onwards. It seemed like they had been in the forest for hours and, truly, they were scared. One of Ben's greater fears was the dark, but he tried not to let this affect him, as he knew Harriet was even more nervous than he was.

What made matters worse for them was that it seemed the small path they were following had faded out and there was no sign of the track Mr Sharpe had spoken of. They had no option but to walk in as straight a line as the forest would allow and were now weaving in and out of thick clumps of trees, coarse carpets of stinging nettles and other more creepy looking areas they did not want to go near.

Together we will endeavour to find the treasure, Ben thought for the hundredth time. Occasionally he would say it out loud in an attempt to keep Harriet's spirits up, and Mr Sharpe's phrase had almost become their slogan. The children were on their own now – for the first time in their mission they had to rely entirely on themselves. Ben had taken his sword out a while ago and regularly had to use it to hit low-lying branches and contorted weeds out of the way as they moved blindly but carefully through the foreboding forest.

Shadows swarmed and squirmed around them, making them feel like they were under constant surveillance, and every time one of them stood on a dead branch they both shot around to see who was behind them. And what were those deep wailing noises in the distance?

They continued to walk on and soon Ben was beginning to think he needed glasses as he struggled to see in the darkness, but when Harriet's grip on his hand relinquished he turned around to face her. He could just make out her hand pointing past him, slightly to the right, and when he turned around he too could see the golden light shimmering in the near distance. Could it be the north of the island, the end of the forest calling them?

Forgetting the tangled knots below and vast trunks around them, they ran as fast as they could towards the light. As they got nearer, though, they saw more dark on the other side and realised they were still deep in the forest. Was it just their imagination then, this golden hope, a mirage in their minds? A few steps further told them: they were in a clearing and golden late afternoon sunlight shone around them. They welcomed the warmth, realising that it had been quite cold in the dark depths they had come from.

'Room to rest,' panted Ben as he came to a halt.

Harriet relaxed a bit in this more welcoming surrounding. They stood there for a while breathing deeply, the tension of the forest momentarily slipping away.

'Can you see any tracks or paths?' asked Harriet. They both started to look around the clearing.

And then it came: the wailing noise they had heard before, but this time much closer. Their eyes shot around them nervously and they pressed together. There was silence once more, but then, in a heartbeat, a chanting sound surrounded them – a chanting of words they understood.

'Whether night or day, it is dark in this place,
And you're not going to get out of here,
We are the creatures of dark and of deep,
We never tire and we never sleep.
In this forest we wait longingly all day,
For the chance to hunt down our prey!'

It was coming from all around them but at the same time it was in their minds, echoing around eerily. Clearly spoken menacing words that sent a chill through the two children.

Confusion set in. Who… what was saying that? Was it the trees? Or was this just a trick their minds were playing on them, like they thought the clearing had been? They stared at each other, their panic growing, but before they had time to think the chanting started again, fiercer and more threatening.

'We are gonna get you,
we're coming for you now,
We're the creatures of the dark,
the deepest fear in you,
You can run but you can't hide,
No way for you to change this tide,
We never tire of what we do,
And what we do is scare you through!'

And as this last chant came, Ben and Harriet spun in confusion, their heads pounding. They were surrounded. Horribly deformed monkey-like beings, each at least six foot tall and covered in disgusting dark matted hair, had appeared out of nowhere, their faces masked by piercing shadow.

Shaking violently at this sudden terror, Harriet tried to let out a scream, but all she could manage was a cracked 'B-Ben!'

Slowly, fearfully, Ben raised his wooden sword and pointed it at the nearest creature, a particularly dark and repulsive monster barely feet away from him. He felt terribly small and the sword dreadfully insignificant as the creature leered at him and let out a sharp, ugly laugh. The laugh quickly became a bloodcurdling wail and the other creatures started laughing and wailing as they all pressed in on the two small children. The sound was unbearable this close and rang harshly through Ben and Harriet's ears, bursting into their minds and filling their whole bodies with fear. They collapsed to the ground, Ben still feebly holding the sword up.

'*You think that puny thing is gonna scare me, boy? Expect me to run away, do ya?*' The high, cold voice filled Ben's head as if it was coming from inside him. He couldn't see the face of the creature that had spoken, if it had a face at all, but he knew it had said those words. As the beast bore down on him, a decaying, sweaty smell made Ben retch. Harriet pressed hard against him. In a sweeping movement the creature whipped away his sword and Ben was defenceless. All he and Harriet could do was huddle together at the centre of the ring of monsters. They were trapped.

'*Children!*' said another voice eagerly.

'*What a waste!*' came a contorted female tone.

'*A little waste, but what a taste.*'

The voices fired through the children, bouncing around the circle, which was becoming darker and darker. The light of the clearing seemed to have been sucked away and they were now in a horrifying shadow land where silhouettes danced over shadows that were not created by light.

'*Shall we eat them?!*'

'*Let's feed our hungry stomachs now.*'

'*And have ourselves a tasty snack!*'

The creatures started to dance around Ben and Harriet, as if engaging in a dark ritual, viciously moving in on them. The dancing got faster and faster and the chanting started again, too frenzied to distinguish what was being said.

As Ben and Harriet thought there was no hope of escaping, another voice rose above the chanting – a voice that was clearly human, coming from outside the circle:

'Be gone, foul creatures of the forest!'

The creatures stopped dancing and froze.

'Move back to your dingy holes, or face my terrible wrath!'

There was sudden chaos. The creatures were fleeing from the clearing, running away from something. Through the confusion the children saw a black figure, not like the creatures, but simply dressed in black, walking towards them, its arms moving in the direction of the remaining creatures.

Before they knew it, Ben and Harriet were being lifted to their feet and found themselves once more in the golden clearing, standing in front of a wrinkled woman dressed in a long black cloak, her grey hair flowing down her back. The creatures were gone.

'Thank you… you s-saved us,' stuttered Harriet, relieved but shaken.

Ben, however, was more suspicious of this woman. 'Why did the creatures run away from you?'

'They know my powers too well.' Her voice showed her to be a lot stronger than her appearance suggested.

'And who are you exactly?'

'My name is Ethel Crabthorn. Some know me as an enigma, some a siren, others a gypsy. However, to you I am simply a woman who has lived in this forest for many years and knows it all too well.'

She seemed to be a normal enough person and even if she did have a bit of an uncertain quality about her, she had saved them from the dinner plates of the Creatures of Shadow.

'So what are two young children such as yourselves doing in the forest on a day like this?' asked Ethel.

'We're trying to get to the north of the island,' said Harriet.

'And we've got a bit lost,' added Ben.

'I see. Well, that is a problem. Would you like me to guide you to where you need to go?'

Ben and Harriet looked at each other. Could they trust Ethel Crabthorn? They were hopelessly lost in the forest and there was nothing else that could help them find their way out – really, they had no choice but to believe that, despite her sudden appearance and the fact that they had only just met her, she genuinely wanted to help them.

'That would be very helpful,' replied Ben, carefully.

'Then follow me, my dears!' Ethel walked towards a small passage carved in between two trees, heading right out of the clearing, and beckoned Ben and Harriet to follow. 'You know, it's very rare we find two such lovely children in the forest. This is a treat.'

With Ethel Crabthorn at the helm, they crept onwards through the forest.

Chapter 11

Discovery

The end of school bell had rung an hour ago at Stormy Cliff; all the children were safely home and Ben and Harriet were still missing. As Mr Harris contemplated where they were, with a lot more concern now, Mrs Davies strode into the classroom. Mr Harris had always known Ben and Harriet's mother to be a kindly woman with a determined smile, but now her face was stricken with worry and more so with anger, and he knew something was definitely wrong.

Unsure of what to say, he stood up behind his desk; Mrs Davies stood breathing heavily a few desks away. Eventually she spoke, unable to control the shake in her voice.

'Where are my children?'

Mr Harris thought for a while, trying to avoid the panicked look he was being given. All he could say was, 'I… I don't know, Mrs Davies.'

'What do you mean, you don't know? I've heard terrible… the most terrible stories. First my husband – who is ill, you know – rings to tell me that my children have been sent to a boarding school for bad behaviour without our permission. Then I hear from Barbara Evans who has seen them on the island and tells me they are off on a treasure hunt! What is going on, Mr Harris?'

The teacher froze, his mind momentarily becoming numb, and then he realised what he had just heard. What had Mr Traiton done to Ben and Harriet?

'Oh no!' he exclaimed. 'I haven't got a clue what's going on. M-Mr Traiton took them out of class this morning and they never returned. I'm… I'm so sorry, Mrs Davies.'

'Mr Traiton took them out of class? So, had they been causing trouble as he told my husband? I need to know what's going on!'

'Yes… yes, so do I. Ben and Harriet have never put a foot out of line. We must go and see Mr Traiton immediately and find out exactly what is happening.' Mr Harris strode to the door. 'Follow me, Mrs Davies.'

* * *

As they approached the heavy oak door of Mr Traiton's office they heard him talking. Mr Harris raised his hand to knock on the door, but Mrs Davies stopped him and they both pressed their ears to the thick wood, listening in to what the head teacher was saying – perhaps it had something to do with Ben and Harriet.

'Yes… yes you will get your money, Ashcroft, don't worry. It's all in good hands.' Mr Traiton's powerful voice was so loud it carried clearly, even through the thick door. He was on the phone. 'Yes, a couple of days, that's all. The factory will be built!'

'A factory? What's this about a factory?' Mrs Davies whispered. Mr Harris shook his head – he didn't know.

'Where's the money coming from? I've told you before, I got two of the pests they call school children to go off on a little treasure hunt for me.'

'He… he means Ben and Harriet, doesn't he?' Mrs Davies's voice sunk. 'Barbara was right, he's sent them into danger!'

'How did I persuade them to do it? I simply told them that if they found the treasure I would use it to save their school. But anyway, when they bring me that treasure I'll convert it into money, with which I will pay you to turn this dump into a steel works factory.'

'Steel works factory!'

'To be honest, I expected the children back a while ago, but they should turn up with the treasure soon, and even if they don't, I can just get more of the pests to go in search of it until the treasure is found… You want proof? I can get you that… Look, Ashcroft, you're a building contractor, not an accountant; you'll get your money in good time. Now if that is all, I'm a busy man, I'll say good day to you.' The head teacher put the phone down. On the other side of the door Mr Harris and Mrs Davies were speechless.

'What… what will happen to me, sir, when the factory is built?' came Mr Foxsworth's nervous voice, much quieter than Mr Traiton's.

'Oh, you'll probably stay on as my assistant, Foxsworth, I don't think I need to get anyone else. And I'll have a perfect workforce to start me off too. Fresh, young, full of energy – finally a decent use for children.'

'He's planning to use the children as his workforce?!' Mr Harris exclaimed; he couldn't comprehend what he was hearing.

'This man is evil… pure evil!' said Mrs Davies heavily, tears filling her eyes. 'What can we do now?'

'Mr Traiton must be stopped, but our first priority has to be to find your children and make sure they are ok,' said Mr Harris.

'We should go to the police. From there we can set up search parties to look for them. Oh Ben, Harriet, my children… where are you…' Her voice tailed off.

'Mrs Davies, you go to the police and arrange those search parties. I am going to go immediately to find Ben and Harriet – they could be in trouble and the sooner we find them the better.'

'Oh, thank you, Mr Harris. Please, find them and… and keep them safe.'

They went their separate ways. Mr Harris dashed back to his classroom, gathered up all the belongings he thought he would need – torches, coat, food and water – and ran out of the school, heading north in his attempt to find his two missing pupils.

CHAPTER 12

A Witch Revealed

Ethel Crabthorn should definitely not have been trusted. She had led Ben and Harriet through the forest, moving deeper into the darkness, but they went nowhere near a track that would lead them to safety, and instead found themselves outside a dilapidated, decaying building. It was lit by one lamp, which glowed an ominous green. This was the last image the two children remembered when they woke up the next morning, trapped inside a rusty metal cage.

The sight that greeted them when they stirred was not a welcoming one. Ben came to first and was able to warn Harriet so that she didn't panic too much. Between the bars of the cage they saw a long, dingy room with a low ceiling, lit by the same green lamps as outside the house. The walls were stone, with a build-up of rot and wet moss that made them look unnaturally slimy in the light. There was one large table in the middle of the room, covered with a mess of bottles, paper, books and strange objects that moved slowly. The smell was dank and musty, the feeling cold.

Huddled close together in the cage, Ben and Harriet shivered as they wondered what had happened to them. After a while they heard footsteps creaking along the floorboards somewhere nearby, and then a voice.

'Ah, awake now are you, children?' said Ethel from a doorway to their right.

She walked towards the cage and peered in at the children, her harsh, wrinkled face showing a greedy smile, her hair now tied in a tight bun.

'We trusted you to help us,' Ben said bitterly.

'Oh and I have, my dear. Those creatures won't be able to touch you in here.'

She ran a long, yellow fingernail slowly down one of the bars of the cage. Harriet shifted uncomfortably beside Ben; he grabbed her hand and held it tightly.

'Where are we?' he asked.

'Oh yes, I forgot to say – welcome to my house. I do very much hope you like it here.' Her voice was sarcastic and showed no sign that she hoped this. She had changed from the nice, normal woman the children had met in the forest to a twisted, evil one. Although Ben felt more scared now than he had ever been before, he let his anger control him and continued to talk.

'No, I don't like it here, it's a foul place.'

'Well, that is a shame, seeing as this could be the last room you will ever see.'

'What do you mean, the last room we will see? Who… who are you?'

'I told you, I am Ethel Crabthorn by name and witch by nature.'

Harriet stared up at the black-cloaked figure, tears welling in her frightened eyes.

'Witch?!' exclaimed Ben. 'You told us you were just a woman of the forest.'

'Well, I am. I'm the witch of the Forest of Shadows. Anyway, enough of this small talk, I have work to do.'

She swept over to the table, sat down and began to search feverishly through the collection of items on it.

'What do we do, Ben?' Harriet whispered weakly.

'I… I don't know. We're trapped… there's no way we can get out of this.'

'Quiet, brat!' Ethel snapped at Ben. 'I'm trying to concentrate here. If I can find the instructions this is going to be the best potion I've ever made, now that I have the *special* ingredients.'

She continued uprooting books and bottles and jars until she came to what she wanted. As she picked up the piece of parchment, which was as old and wrinkled as she was, she gave the children a menacing stare.

'Perfect. I've always wanted to try this one. If I get it right the potion will be ready for tomorrow and then we can set about our plans.'

Ben and Harriet stared at each other – they were locked in a cage in a witch's house as she contemplated her next potion; it was clear that they had something to do with it, that they were the special ingredients. In desperation Ben tried tugging at the bars of the cage. It made an awful racket.

'Stop that, boy, or I'll cut your fingers off!'

Ben withdrew his hands quickly. 'Isn't that what you're going to do anyway?'

'I don't know, I haven't looked at the ingredients yet. What would you prefer it to be, your hands or your tongue?'

She returned to the piece of parchment and began to pick items up at random, according to what she read.

'So, what's so special about this potion then?' Ben asked, thinking quickly – if he could distract her in some way perhaps that would give them a way out.

'Why should I tell you?' Ethel glowered. 'Well, I might as well I suppose. This potion, when mixed properly, will turn the sweetest, nicest person into an evil beast. There may only be me and my sister left, but with enough beasts to do our bidding we'll be able to take over this whole island!'

'Why can't you use the creatures from the forest? They seemed pretty evil.'

'We need intelligence, boy! What is the point of evil if it isn't intelligent? Those creatures couldn't tell a tree stump from a sheep.'

'So that's it, is it? You're just going to kill us?'

'That remains to be seen; I must find my other ingredients first. Now be quiet!' She turned away from the cage and back to her search.

'I'm sorry, Harriet, so sorry,' said Ben.

'There's n-nothing we could have done,' his sister replied.

'But I'm the one who said we should go on this journey. It's my fault we're here.'

'No, you can't s-say that, Ben, it's nobody's fault but Mr Traiton's. He sent us to get the treasure.' She put her arms around him and they hugged.

So this was it – they had set out to find treasure and their short lives would end here, in the Forest of Shadows. No one would ever know what had happened to them and they would never see their parents or friends again. Quietly, they cried together.

As Ethel clattered around the room there was a knock on the front door, which was at the other end of the room to Ben and Harriet. The witch let go of the cauldron she was dragging out from under the table, grunted and strode over to the door, opening it fiercely.

'Yes?' she demanded. 'This better be good or you're for it!'

'I… I have been asked to inform you by… by the Thistlewick magistrates' court that your sister, Gladys, has been arrested and is to appear in court in one hour.' Although Ben and Harriet could only just hear the voice of the man who spoke, it sounded very familiar. But surely it couldn't be…

'What?!' said Ethel loudly.

'Your sister is to appear in court in one hour and… and has requested you as a witness.'

'Oh newts! I can't have this, not with the plans we can put in place tomorrow!'

Without a second thought the witch stormed out of the house, leaving the door open behind her. A few moments later the man cautiously entered the room.

'Mr Harris!' screamed Harriet, and Ben had to hold his sister down to keep her from banging her head on the top of the cage.

'Harriet, Ben? Oh thank goodness you're safe.'

'How did you…' Ben began.

'No time to explain now,' Mr Harris interrupted. 'The witch could be back at any minute. Is there a key to unlock you?'

'I… I don't know.'

'I'll have to look then.' Mr Harris turned to the table and started throwing its contents onto the floor in his hurry to find a key. Bottles smashed and thick liquids seeped out, releasing strong odours that made them all feel sick.

'Mr Harris!' cried Harriet. 'Over there.'

She was pointing to a place on the wall between two of the lamps, where a large ring hung on a rusty nail; on the ring was a key. Mr Harris grabbed hold of it, ran over to the cage and, after fumbling with the key for a few seconds, was able to fit it into the lock and turn it. With a loud creak the cage split in half and the children stepped out.

'Thank you, Mr Harris, thank you!' said Harriet, overcome with joy.

The teacher turned towards the door.

'Come on,' he said. 'Let's get out of here.'

CHAPTER 13

Half Acre Farm

'So, is Gladys really in court?' asked Harriet.

They had escaped from the forest with no more delays and were now sitting in a field of long grass on the north of the island, with sunlight dazzling their eyes and cows grazing behind them. It was an unbelievable relief to be out in the fresh air, and this feeling filled Ben and Harriet with energy. Mr Harris, though, looked exhausted.

'No,' he replied. 'I made that up – Thistlewick doesn't have a courtroom anymore.'

'How did you know that Gladys was that witch's sister?' asked Ben. 'No one knows anything about her.'

'I remembered a conversation I had with the vicar the first time I encountered Gladys. He said he had heard rumours that she was a witch and lived with her sister in the forest. Of course, neither of us believed that – we thought witches were a thing of the past – but when I saw the house in the forest, and then as she opened the door, I just knew the rumours were true.'

'That was very quick thinking to come up with that story, sir,' said Ben.

'Thank you. Now, please tell me, did Mr Traiton send you two on a mission to find him treasure?'

'Yes,' said Harriet. 'Didn't you know?'

'He wants us to find the treasure that will save Stormy Cliff,' explained Ben.

'Well, I'm afraid that's not exactly the case,' said Mr Harris. 'Let me tell you what's been going on…'

He explained to the children that he and their mother had heard Mr Traiton discussing his plans to use the treasure to turn Stormy Cliff into a steel works factory. He told them how he had set off to find them while their mother arranged search parties, that Mr Sharpe had told him what was going on, that he had climbed a tree in the forest to avoid the Creatures of Shadow and stayed there all night until they were gone, and then how he had stumbled across the witch's house and feared the worst.

'But you got us out. You saved us!' Harried smiled.

'I'm terribly sorry that Mr Traiton got you two involved in his evil plans. It must be horrible finding out the truth.'

'To be honest, I think we're just glad to be safe now,' said

Ben. 'He really is evil though – worse than that witch. So what are we going to do now, sir?'

'Well, it depends. Does the treasure really exist?'

'Yes, we're sure it does,' said Harriet. 'The vicar gave us the name of the ship it came from, Tormenta, and the fishermen told us all about it. Mr Gailsborough drew us this map.' She pulled the map out of her bag and showed it to Mr Harris. 'It's just there, in Stowaway Cove.'

'Right, well in that case I feel we have two options. My head tells me that I should take you two straight back home to safety. However, Stormy Cliff really is in danger of being closed down and my heart tells me we should go after this treasure and take it back to the police. Then they will be able to arrest Mr Traiton and we may get some of the treasure to help save Stormy Cliff.'

'Which shall we do then?' asked Ben.

'You two are the true adventurers here. This is your mission, so I will leave the decision up to you.'

Harriet looked at Ben and smiled. 'I think we should find the treasure.'

'Yes,' said Ben. 'We've come this far, so let's get that gold and save Stormy Cliff!'

'Right.' Mr Harris stood up. 'I've only been to the north of Thistlewick once before and I don't know exactly where to go, so the first thing will be to get some directions. There must be a farmhouse around here somewhere; which farm was it that Mr Sharpe told you to go to?'

'That'd be Half Acre, wouldn't it?' said an unfamiliar voice from behind them. A man dressed in rough jeans and a chequered shirt was leaning over a fence, his tufted hair making him look quite comical.

'Mr Potts?' enquired Harriet. She thought she recognised him because Mr Potts's nephew, Kieran, had that same tufted hairstyle.

'That's me all right, and this here field is part of Half Acre Farm. Welcome. How may I be of assistance?'

'We're looking for Stowaway Cove,' said Mr Harris.

'Hummm. I can't say I recognise that name. There's a good deal of coves over on the northeast side, perhaps it's one of them?'

'We have this,' said Harriet, showing him the map. 'And we think we're heading for that cross.'

'Ah ok, I know where you have to go,' said Mr Potts. 'This map isn't very detailed, is it? I'll fill it in a bit for you.' He pulled a pen from his shirt pocket and drew another cross. 'You are here, and you need to get to Watcher's Cliff, so if you head this way out of Half Acre, go straight through Fairfield's Farm and then east through the corn fields of Manor Farm; that'll get you there. Then, you see this dip here in your map, where the cross is, that'll be Stowaway Cove to the right of Watcher's Cliff.' He drew an outline of each farm and the route they had to take onto the map as he talked.

'Thank you very much, that's a great help,' said Mr Harris.

'You know, all my life, I've never known that that cove was called Stowaway,' said Mr Potts.

'Well, as a teacher, I have to say, you learn something new every day. Right, we must be off, come on you two.'

The children waved at the farmer as they walked off through the long grass, smiling. Everything was going right.

'Oh, and the cows say that you'll have good weather all the way,' Mr Potts called after them.

CHAPTER 14

Stowaway Cove

Ben and Harriet had always thought the best view from Thistlewick could be seen from the path behind their house, where the lines of trees cleared and the land opened up to reveal a magnificent view of a majestic sea, which shimmered turquoise on a good day. However, what they saw now, as they looked out over Watcher's Cliff, far surpassed this image. Below them was the rugged edge of the dark cliff with small white waves crashing into its bottom; further out to sea the waves became taller and more powerful, creating a vast and impressive view. Sharp edged rocks occasionally broke up the deep blue of the sea and as waves crashed into them, eddies formed in the wake.

Mr Harris also found the view stunning, but as the children stared out off the north of the island, he regained his bearings and looked at the map. He found where they were and, glancing down to his right, saw the cove that was represented on the map by a dip with a cross in it.

'Stowaway Cove is down to our right,' he said.

Harriet's eyes shot to the right and lit up. 'You mean we're almost there? Actually almost there?'

'Yes.'

'Well, what are we waiting for?' Ben exclaimed as he started to run towards the edge of the cliff.

'Careful Ben, don't run,' Mr Harris warned. 'Remember, you are on top of a cliff and that's a hundred foot drop.'

'Sorry, I just got carried away.'

'Let's leave getting carried away until after we've found the treasure. Now, it looks like we'll have to climb down this cliff, so we must be very cautious and take it slowly. I'll go first and you two follow directly behind me.'

Mr Harris stepped off the top of the cliff and started to climb down, using the jagged edges of the rock as foot and hand holes. Harriet went next, followed closely by Ben, and carefully the three of them descended into Stowaway Cove. They landed on thick golden sand, which showed no signs of having been touched by humans for many years, and soon their feet sank in and the sand wrapped around them as if welcoming a new friend.

The cove was rectangular in shape and divided up by layers of granite grey rock. It seemed quite peaceful at the moment, with the deep hum of the sea and intermittent gull cries being the only sounds they could hear. With the sun high in the sky and a gentle breeze blowing, the children couldn't imagine a ship being wrecked here.

As the tide started to go out, though, a series of pointed rocks revealed themselves, almost in a semi-circle around the cove; these were soon joined by more rocks leading out into the deep sea. It was clear now that any ship unlucky enough to head here on a stormy night and not see the rocks would meet a very sudden, sharp ending – even a ship as great as the Tormenta.

'It's a shame we had to tell the fishermen this was only a school research project,' said Ben. 'It would have been so much easier if they had just brought us here by boat – we could have been home by yesterday afternoon.'

'It's a good job we weren't that quick, otherwise we'd have taken the treasure straight back to Mr Traiton,' said Harriet. 'Anyway, the fishermen would never have come to Stowaway Cove; they're too scared of it, aren't they?'

'Oh, and why is that?' asked Mr Harris.

'They told us a story about how the crew of the Tormenta have guarded over their treasure ever since the ship sank,' replied Ben.

'Ah, a fisherman's tale,' said Mr Harris knowingly. 'Yes, I've heard many of them – they're all a bit far fetched and should be taken with a pinch of salt really. So, where is the treasure supposed to be – not on the ship itself still? I can't see any signs of a wreck around here.'

'No, it should be in a cave,' said Harriet.

'Like that one over there?' Mr Harris pointed to a black hole carved into the rock to their left, behind a large build-up of smaller rocks. 'That looks like a cave to me.'

'Let's try it,' said Ben, and they walked over to the left hand side of the cove.

'Here Ben, take a torch – we'll need light in there.'

Mr Harris took two torches out of his bag and gave one to Ben. They climbed over the collection of small rocks and through the dark entrance into the cave.

CHAPTER 15

The Cave

They felt their way along the narrow passage in the pitch black; the sound of the sea outside quickly disappeared and silence surrounded them. The entrance to the cave was damp underfoot and the three adventurers had to grip the sides with their hands to avoid slipping.

When he couldn't feel the rough rock around him anymore, Mr Harris turned on his torch and Ben followed suit. Even with this light, it took a while for their eyes to adjust to the dim of the cave and they could only see a few feet in front of them. Shining the torches around, it seemed they were in a large dome-shaped space with a high ceiling. The air was musty.

'Right, let's find this treasure,' said Mr Harris, his voice carrying around the cave and coming back in a loud echo. 'You two have a look around to the right; I'll go to the left. Be careful now.'

'Do you think we're looking for a chest?' Ben asked his sister.

'I don't know, but whatever it is, it'll be obvious,' Harriet replied.

The children began to walk around the right hand side of the cave, following the rocky edge. This was an important situation now and they took it seriously – they could afford to be excited once the treasure was safely outside.

Mr Harris set off to his left and walked cautiously, shining his torch around in search of any objects that weren't rocks. Looking over to where Ben and Harriet were, he could just see the faint beam of light emanating from their torch.

All of a sudden a high-pitched scream shot around the cave.

'Harriet!' called Ben.

'What's happened?' shouted Mr Harris. He felt something rush past him like a cold wind and swung his torch around. Nothing was there. 'Is Harriet ok, Ben?'

'She's… she's gone. She's not here.'

More wind-like sensations rushed past Ben and Mr Harris, chilling them through. They built up and became faster and faster, creating a whirlwind of air around the cave.

'The girl is safe,' said a loud, bone-chilling voice.

'What was that? Who's there?' said Mr Harris. He couldn't tell where the voice had come from because it filled the whole cave at once.

There was a flash of light like a firework in a small space, which exploded around the cave. As it cleared, Mr Harris and Ben saw a figure illuminated by a clear, bright light, a distance away from them at the end of the cave. The figure was a large man, dressed in grand, blood-red clothing and wearing a wide brimmed hat. There was something about him that wasn't quite there, almost as if he were being projected onto the rock where he sat; his presence, though, felt overwhelming.

'Where's Harriet?' Ben shouted. 'Where's my sister?'

The man gestured behind Ben, who turned around and with a jump saw Harriet in the tight grip of another man, who was wearing a shabby shirt and a red headband. The man grinned inanely and shone in the same bright light as the man in the wide brimmed hat.

'Get off her! Let go of her!' Ben cried.

'Release her, Brownjohn, she's only a child,' said the man in the wide brimmed hat. Brownjohn let go of his captive and Harriet ran over to Ben, clinging onto him tightly.

'Who are you?' asked Mr Harris.

'I am Captain Roger Traiton.'

'Pirates!' gasped Harriet. 'Ben, the ghosts! It's t-true!'

'Ah, so you haven't just stumbled upon this cave then. You know of our story – that of the great Tormenta,' said Captain Traiton. His voice was deep and formidably powerful. 'Men, come out. These people know our story, let us greet them properly.'

And out of nowhere they came, many more men, wearing a variety of ragged clothing and glowing menacingly – the pirate crew of the Tormenta. The light that came with them filled the cave more than any natural light could. They stood keenly around Ben, Harriet and Mr Harris, staring at them greedily.

Mr Harris tried to run over to the children – he had to protect them – but he was held back by one of the pirates; the grip on his arm was icy cold and sent a shock through his body.

'And how do we greet our guests, men?' said Captain Traiton.

The crew let out a loud, foreboding cheer, as if they had just won a battle over a great enemy. The cave seemed to spark and the light intensified.

'Well, I bet you didn't think we existed, did you?' the captain asked.

Neither Mr Harris nor the children spoke – they were too frightened for words.

'Did you?' his voice was more forceful.

'N-no,' stuttered Mr Harris.

'That's right. You heard our story – the tale of how the greatest ship ever to be built came to an end off these shores – and you probably thought it was just an old tale of ghosts contrived to scare away the keen adventurer. But the mention of treasure, no doubt, made you desperate to visit this cave. And so you came, and here you are now – trapped by the ghost crew of the Tormenta.'

'We need the treasure to save our school!' said Harriet, without thinking. Surprised by the sound of her own voice, she sank back into her brother.

'To save your school, ay,' said Captain Traiton, with a hint of bitterness in his voice. 'Well, I have to say that when me and this group of murderous scallywags here left our bodies with the sea, and when we brought our treasure into this here cave to guard forever from those who try to take it, I don't think we ever considered using it to save a mere school.'

'And we never will!' cried Brownjohn.

'Aye! This treasure is ours, nobody else's!' The captain moved his hand to his side and patted a chest. The treasure chest. It was large and carved in dark wood, with a brilliant golden rim.

The children's hearts sank – there was no chance of getting the treasure now and they knew their lives were in great danger. Terrified, they looked over to Mr Harris and he stared back at them across the cave, anguish filling his face.

CHAPTER 16

Mr Traiton's Lesson

'Aren't you meant to be teaching us, sir?' asked Jack.

Mr Traiton gave him a dirty glare from the front of the class, where he was slumped lazily in Mr Harris's chair.

'Teach you, boy! You don't know the meaning of the word education.'

'We would if we had a dictionary,' piped up Rebecca.

The head teacher stood up angrily. 'Why, you impudent little…'

'Leave her alone!' Jimmy interrupted, quite to everyone's surprise. He was sitting bolt upright in his chair.

'Quiet, boy! You children, you don't know a thing. We had the cane back in my day and if I was allowed you'd have all had it by now.'

Various members of the class let out gasps, others kept quiet, but they were all shocked. Mr Traiton was even crueller than they had thought.

'Very well, seeing as your stupid excuse for a teacher, Mr Harris, has decided to run off and leave me to deal with you, I'll give you a lesson. Have you ever heard of a steel works factory?'

The class mumbled quietly, taking great insult to how the head teacher had described Mr Harris. Mr Traiton took this as a 'no' to his question.

'Well you'll know about steel works factories soon enough,' he said. 'You lucky blighters, you won't know what's hit you. A school education doesn't get you anywhere these days, but that won't matter once you're working in my factory.'

'Factory?' questioned Jack.

'Yes, factory. You'll be perfect for the job. Now take this lad here.' He grabbed Jimmy from the front row and pulled him viciously up to the front of the class. 'He's young with no brains, but quite able bodied. An excellent steel worker.'

'But I want to be an astronaut,' said Jimmy, earnestly.

'You'll never be an astronaut; you don't deserve to be an astronaut. If you don't work for me I'll see that you never work at all. Sit down. Now, I'm a busy man and I'm not going to stand here lecturing you lot all day. You can start writing out your job applications. Someone hand paper round. I expect four sides before the end of today.'

Mr Traiton dropped back down into the chair at the front of the class as the children reluctantly began to carry out his tasks in shocked silence.

CHAPTER 17

The Fight

'I bet you're regretting your decision to steal my treasure now, aren't you? Thought you'd get it easily, didn't you?' said Captain Traiton slyly.

Ben, Harriet and Mr Harris were becoming more and more trapped. They wished they could crumble into nothing under the pressure of the pirates around them.

'Well, let me give you a glimpse of hope, like the kind-hearted captain I am. I shall challenge you to a duel for the treasure, as I have all the other fools who have tried to take it from me…'

The pirate crew let out another ferocious cheer.

'Quiet, you rabble!' called the captain. There was immediate silence. 'You will fight for the treasure and your freedom. The rules are simple: if you win, you can take the treasure and go, but if I win, you do not get the treasure and you die.' He grinned cruelly at his captives. 'I must warn you though – I have never been defeated by any person, living or dead; in fact, the only thing that has ever triumphed over me is the sea. So, which one of you is going to try to best me?'

'We're only children!' Ben pleaded.

'I will,' said Mr Harris, quietly. 'I will fight you.'

'Mr Harris, no!' cried Harriet.

'I must Harriet, there's no other way.'

It was true – they were in an impossible situation and this was their only chance to get out alive, however unlikely it seemed.

'Oh and how very brave of you,' said Captain Traiton sarcastically. 'Very well. What is your name, sir?'

'Andrew Harris.'

'Well, Mr Harris, we fight with swords, but I don't suppose you have one. Fletcher, give him your sword.'

The pirate named Fletcher, who stood nearest to Mr Harris, pulled his sword from his belt and thrust it begrudgingly at him. As its hard silver edge shone in the light, it was clear there was nothing ghostly about the sword, and Mr Harris saw the terror in his own eyes reflected in its sharp blade.

Captain Traiton stood up and pulled his sword out – it was far superior to Mr Harris's in both size and brilliance and glinted blindingly. He stepped down from the rock on which he had sat with the treasure chest and moved slowly towards Mr Harris, each step more forceful than the last. He reached the teacher and stared into his eyes. Mr Harris wanted to recoil in fear, but with a great effort he stood his ground.

The captain had an aggressive face covered in many large scars; his hair was matted under his hat and his stone-cold eyes were piercing in their darkness. Continuing to stare Mr Harris out, he shouted an order to his crew:

'Men, surround the children. Don't let them escape – I want them to see this.'

The crew swept over to Ben and Harriet and surrounded them in a semi-circle to one corner of the cave. The children were trapped and struggled to see what was happening – the ghosts weren't at all transparent. Looking around them they could just see the treasure chest illuminated to their right and Mr Harris and Captain Traiton ahead of them, about to fight. They huddled together and waited for the worst to happen.

'I hope you are prepared to die, Mr Harris!' said Captain Traiton viciously.

He raised his sword and Mr Harris feebly did the same. The teacher felt his heart beating heavily in his chest and all around his body. He was so scared that it was a struggle even to stand. Perhaps it would be easier to just fall down and give in. No, he had to fight. For the children, he had to fight. But how could he defeat a ghost?

Captain Traiton swung his sword and somehow Mr Harris managed to lift his own weapon up in front of him in defence. The two swords met with a great crash of metal and the collision sent a sharp vibration up Mr Harris's arm, causing him to yelp in pain. Before he had time to recover the captain swung a second blow and he blocked again. And again.

Behind the other pirates, Ben and Harriet could hear the great clang of metal on metal and Mr Harris's cries of pain. Harriet screwed up her eyes as Ben turned away. Mr Harris would lose – he didn't stand a chance.

'You'll never win you know,' said Captain Traiton airily. 'No one ever wins against the great Captain Traiton.'

The crew jeered from their spectator's position. Mr Harris didn't respond – it was too much to defend himself let alone talk.

Smash! Crash! Pain. Bash! Clunk! Crunch! Agony. The sword fight, which was only ever one sided, went on. It would only be a matter of time before Captain Traiton finished Mr Harris off – he was merely teasing his prey and everyone in the cave knew it.

There has to be something I can do to help, thought Ben as he became more and more desperate. He felt so pathetic just standing there unable to do anything. Then an idea came to him – there was only a very slim chance it might work, but in this situation anything was worth a try.

The pirates' concentration was clearly on the fight and Ben took his bag off his back and opened it. He rummaged around and all he could find was his water bottle. Taking it out, he bent down to the ground and managed to position himself so that he could just see the duellers between the legs of two pirates. He knew he would only have one chance at this and his aim and timing had to be perfect. With his heart in his mouth, Ben placed the bottle lengthways on the ground, lined up his shot and rolled it carefully through the gap he had found.

The bottle moved slowly along the ground and went unnoticed by the cheering pirates. It got nearer and nearer to Captain Traiton, and just as his sword narrowly missed Mr Harris's arm and he lunged forward for another strike, the bottle stopped in front of his right foot, and he tripped on it and fell. Mr Harris jumped out of the way as the captain landed heavily on the ground.

Chaos broke out amongst the pirates as they all ran towards Mr Harris and Captain Traiton. Only Brownjohn had the sense to stay behind and held Ben back.

'No! Leave him – he's mine!' cried Captain Traiton as the pirates crowded around Mr Harris. 'Go on then, Harris, do it. Stab me!'

Mr Harris was frozen to the spot – he didn't know what to do.

Harriet was now staring wide-eyed at the pirates surrounding Mr Harris, but Ben, seeing she was free, whispered in her ear, 'Harriet, run for the treasure. Now! Run.'

She quickly sprang into action and ran towards the chest. In a flash Brownjohn realised what was happening and charged after her, his sword raised. Ben ran forwards and grabbed a sword from one of the pirates, who was too engrossed in the fight to notice it being taken. Ben sprinted towards Brownjohn and caught up with him. They swung their swords at each other and connected with a resounding clang!

Mr Harris was still motionless, glued to the ground. Captain Traiton and the crew were now laughing at him. He never thought he would be in this position, having to face up to killing someone. Then he realised – Captain Traiton was a ghost, he had nothing to lose. Lifting his sword high in the air he plunged it downwards.

Harriet was almost at the chest. Ben and Brownjohn were now fighting seriously, but as Mr Harris made his move, they both paused to look.

For a moment, Mr Harris thought he had succeeded in defeating Captain Traiton as the sword moved cleanly into his stomach. But the pirates only laughed louder.

'You really think it would be that easy?' said Captain Traiton cruelly.

And as Mr Harris pulled his sword out he saw a horrifying sight – the blade, which had been so solid and strong a second ago, was slowly disintegrating. Suddenly there was nothing left but the hilt that Mr Harris held in his hand. He stood there speechless and swordless.

'Handy being a ghost,' Captain Traiton said. 'Gives you special powers. Like I said, you can't win.'

The captain stood up to his full height in front of Mr Harris once more. As he did, he saw Harriet at the treasure chest, trying to get it open, and his own panic set in.

'The girl! You fools, you let her escape! The girl! She's at the chest. Get her!'

At this command the crew turned and, seeing what was happening, charged towards Harriet. She was struggling desperately with the lock on the chest, but couldn't get it to open.

Captain Traiton pounced on Mr Harris and knocked him to the ground.

'And you,' he said, 'this is the end of you.' He raised his sword.

The pirates charged towards Harriet with their swords raised and were half way there. Seeing his sister was struggling, Ben threw his sword into the air in her direction. As it flew, as if in slow motion, it passed through Brownjohn's chest and then through two more pirates who were in its path. It continued on its journey towards Harriet and the chest, but Ben knew it would disintegrate.

'Harriet, get the sword and stab the chest!' he shouted at the top of his voice. 'Quick, before it disappears!'

The sword bounced and landed on the floor between Harriet and the oncoming pirates. She ran towards it, grabbed hold and dived towards the chest before the pirates caught up with her. The sword plunged into the dark wood.

A silence filled the cave as the pirates realised what had just happened.

'Nooooooo!' came a bone-chilling cry that belonged to Captain Traiton, who stood motionless over Mr Harris. As his voice echoed through the cave, the chest slowly started to crumble.

There was a sudden rush of wind and the pirates were rapidly swept towards the remains of the chest. Harriet shielded herself against the wall as the pirates soared towards her. The light around the chest became brighter and brighter and as Captain Traiton flew uncontrollably forward, his cries went with him. The light became a blinding white and Ben was knocked off his feet by the force of the wind.

There was a loud explosion and the cave was plunged into darkness.

CHAPTER 18

Treasure

Ben staggered to his feet. Regaining his balance, he flicked his torch on.

'Harriet? Mr Harris? Are you there?' he asked cautiously.

'I'm over here,' came Harriet's faint voice.

'I'm here,' came Mr Harris's, and Ben felt his teacher's hand rest upon his shoulder.

The two of them moved over to where Harriet's voice had come from and as they got nearer to her, objects glinted and shimmered in front of them. Ben ran and as he reached Harriet he hugged her. They both looked to their side as Ben shone the torch onto a big pile of magnificent gold.

'You did it, Harriet! You… you actually did it!' he exclaimed.

Harriet stared open-mouthed, unable to comprehend what had just happened. Mr Harris walked up to them and gasped.

'Well I never. Treasure!' He spoke with a mixture of joy, relief and exhaustion.

'W-what just happened?' Harriet asked weakly.

'I don't know,' replied Ben. 'The stories were true. The pirates were real. But we beat them. We've got the treasure!'

'Well done, you two, well done.' Mr Harris sat down next to the children and slowly brushed his shaking hand over a piece of gold.

'Mr Harris, you were so brave,' said Harriet. 'Fighting Captain Traiton like that.'

'If it wasn't for your quick thinking I would have died,' said Mr Harris.

'And if it wasn't for you we would have died,' said Ben.

'We did it together,' smiled Harriet.

'A true team effort,' smiled Mr Harris.

They sat there for what seemed like an age, breathing heavily, letting the mixed feelings run through them. Then in silence they stood up and started examining the treasure. It was a huge collection, much more than the chest could ever have held. It shone brilliantly, as if all the light that had filled the cave moments before had been sucked into it.

There were many gold coins of varying sizes and scattered amongst them were gems and diamonds of all colours, set in necklaces and rings and other grand objects.

'So, what are we going to do?' asked Ben.

'We'll have to fill our bags with as much of this as we can, I suppose,' said Mr Harris.

'But we won't be able to carry all that,' said Harriet.

And it was true, they couldn't – the three of them packed what would fit into their bags and even stuffed their pockets full to burst, but still at least half of the treasure was left scattered on the ground.

'We'll have to send people back for the rest,' said Mr Harris. 'Come on, let's get out of here, I am in serious need of fresh air.'

* * *

The light of the midday sun blinded the three adventurers as they stepped out of the cave. Stowaway Cove was exactly how they had found it before, with a calm sea, a blue sky and a cool breeze, which gently blew away all their tensions.

'Ben, Harriet, Mr Harris!' came the voice of Ernie the fisherman, as they moved out into the cove.

'Oh, thank goodness you're safe. We've been so worried about you,' said Ted, and he, Ernie and Albert walked up the cove from their boat at the edge of the water. 'Your mother's been so worried about you two. There are search parties looking for you all over the island, like nothing I've seen before.'

'Your mother came and told us what was going on,' said Ernie. 'And of course we knew you'd try to get here after what we told you, so we had to brave up to coming round here ourselves. We just prayed you'd be safe.'

'Thank you,' said Mr Harris.

'So what on earth has happened?' asked Ted.

'The story you told us, about the ghost pirates in the cave, it was true,' said Ben. 'And Mr Harris had to fight the captain and…'

Ben gave the fishermen a detailed account of what he remembered happening, and Harriet chipped in too. It was only now that they realised the enormity of what they had achieved.

'Well, I'll be blowed,' said Ted, open-mouthed. 'So we were right to fear venturing to Stowaway Cove. I never thought… well, I'm lost for words…'

'I have battled the strongest storms and the most ferocious seas,' Albert spoke for the first time. 'I've come close to drowning many times. But what you've done today has shown seven oceans more courage than I ever could.'

They all smiled and enjoyed the moment before Mr Harris remembered the purpose of their quest.

'We need to get this treasure back to the south of the island,' he said.

'Well, let's get going then,' said Ernie. 'We can take you back in the boat. Do you have all the treasure with you?'

'No, there's more back in the cave. If you could come and help us get it. Don't worry, the pirates are all gone –

there's nothing that can harm you in there now,' Mr Harris added, seeing the fishermen's hesitation.

They all went to get the rest of the treasure from the cave and then set off in the boat around Thistlewick, back to the village. The journey took half an hour – somewhat faster than it had taken to get to Stowaway Cove and the treasure – and the children enjoyed it thoroughly.

When they reached the harbour, they placed the gold safely in the hut and Mr Harris, Ben and Harriet gave their thanks to the fishermen and headed straight for the police station. As they approached the tall, grand building they saw a collection of people gathered under its arched entrance. Mr Sharpe was there, the vicar, Miss Susan, Mrs Evans and a variety of other villagers. They all jumped in surprise as they saw the three adventurers approaching.

'Mrs Davies! Mrs Davies!' the vicar called excitedly, and through the congregation came the children's mother. When she saw Ben and Harriet, all worry cleared from her face and she ran forwards to hug them tightly.

'My children! Ben, Harriet, you're safe. Mr Harris you saved my children, thank you. Oh, bless you all. What a relief!' The words tumbled out of her mouth and she began to cry.

'Mum, we've got to see Sergeant Radley,' said Ben, as his mother squeezed him tightly.

'Yes, of course. Of course you do,' she said, letting go of him and Harriet.

They walked determinedly into the police station, followed by Mr Harris.

CHAPTER 19

The Fall of Mr Traiton

'Sir, lunch was meant to start half an hour ago,' said Jack, the first of the class brave enough to raise this point.

Without a word, Mr Traiton rose from the chair at the front of the room and strode to the back, where Jack sat. Towering over him, the head teacher stared malevolently down.

'Lunch. You think you deserve lunch? Well, let me see what you've written then.' He pulled the sheet of paper up from Jack's desk and glanced at the half page of writing. 'No, you're not getting any lunch. In fact none of you will eat anything until Jack here has written four full pages.' Mr Traiton glanced spitefully around the silent children, smiled to himself and walked back to the front.

'But that's not fair!' Jack spoke again.

Mr Traiton spun around and in a flash he was at Jack's desk once more, his face contorted menacingly. The other children let out a gasp as Jack froze. The head teacher grabbed hold of his collar and pulled him up from his seat. Their faces were barely inches apart.

'Not fair? How dare you?' Mr Traiton spat. 'You'll pay for that, you little…'

'Mr Traiton! Leave that child alone!'

'Ah, Sergeant Radley. To what do I owe this pleasure?' Mr Traiton's voice had suddenly turned into a calm, polite one as he realised that the sergeant and his tall deputy, Constable Ockly, were standing in the doorway. He slowly let go of Jack. 'I was just helping this boy here with his work. Oh and Mr Harris, how nice to see you again.'

At the mention of their teacher's name, the class spun around and saw him walking through the doorway behind the policemen, followed by Ben and Harriet.

'Ben!' called William.

'Harriet!' called Catherine.

'Mr Harris!' called Jimmy.

'Ah, children,' Mr Traiton said to Ben and Harriet. 'Do you have anything for me?'

'Ben and Harriet have nothing to give you,' said Mr Harris.

Mr Traiton glared from the children to their teacher.

'Tristan Traiton,' said Sergeant Radley, stepping forward. 'I am arresting you for conspiracy to pervert the course of education. You do not have to…'

'What!' Mr Traiton interrupted, his voice turning angry again. 'This is an outrage! After all I've done for this school! You have no right to arrest me.'

'We know what you were planning to do with that treasure,' said Constable Ockly.

Mr Traiton froze, all argument fading away from him. His plans were uncovered and he was trapped. Constable Ockly moved in to handcuff him and then proceeded to the door, with Mr Traiton writhing and fighting at his side.

'Take your hands off me, you stupid idiot. Why! Why!' the former head teacher shouted. As they reached the door Mr Traiton forced himself around to face Mr Harris, ripping his dark suit in the process. 'Harris, you'll pay for what you've done! I'm coming for you!'

'I don't think that's very likely, sir,' said Constable Ockly.

And with that, Mr Traiton and his evil plans were gone.

'We'll leave you to clear up here then, Mr Harris,' said Sergeant Radley.

'Thank you,' said Mr Harris.

'Oh and the treasure,' said the sergeant. 'I think it belongs to the school now. I'll have it sent round in due course. Use it for a better cause than Traiton was going to.'

'Of course,' said Mr Harris. He let out a wide smile, which was shared by Ben and Harriet.

'It looks like you're in charge now, sir,' said Ben, as Sergeant Radley left the room.

'It would appear so,' said Mr Harris, and he turned to face the class as a whole. 'Children, we're safe. It looks like everything is going to be ok from now on. So let's turn this school around and give you the education you deserve!'

The children clapped and cheered enthusiastically.

'But now I think you all need your lunch,' Mr Harris continued. 'It's a lovely day outside, so why don't you go out to the playground. I'll leave it to Ben and Harriet to explain what's been going on.'

The children all got up and filed past Ben, Harriet and Mr Harris, exchanging grins as they went.

'You two coming?' William asked Ben and Harriet as he passed them.

'We'll be out in a minute,' replied Ben.

'What are you waiting for, go and enjoy some time with your friends,' said Mr Harris, but the two children had a question.

'Mr Harris, how did *we* manage to get the treasure?' asked Harriet. 'Why not any of the other people who tried?'

The teacher thought for a while – it was a question on his mind too. 'Well, Harriet, we can never know. But perhaps the other people who tried to claim the treasure wanted it out of greed. Even the pirates only wanted it out of greed. We needed it to save Stormy Cliff and for the good of everyone here. That, I think, made us a lot more powerful.'

'And we worked together, as a team,' said Ben.

'Exactly,' said Mr Harris. 'I'm not sure the pirates expected that. Now go on, go and talk to your friends – they've been worried about you.'

And Ben and Harriet walked out into the glorious sunlight to answer the many questions that their classmates had for them.

CHAPTER 20

The Rise of Stormy Cliff

'Hurry up, Ben, or you'll make us late!' shouted Mrs Davies, with an exasperated look shared by her husband, who was standing next to her at the front door. It was the first time he had been well enough to move out of the house.

'Thank you for coming with us, Dad,' said Harriet, who was standing just outside the door, her hair in two perfect plaits.

'Well, I couldn't go missing your big day now, could I?' he replied. Today was the official re-opening of Stormy Cliff School and the start of a new term.

A lot had happened since Ben, Harriet and Mr Harris had uncovered the treasure. The Christmas holidays had been extended to allow for the rebuild of Stormy Cliff, and Ben and Harriet had spent the time getting back into normal life again. They had great fun playing with William, Catherine and the others, adventuring all over the south of the island – Harriet with a new sense of confidence. Their mother had gone with them to help decorate the Christmas tree at the church and the Davies family Christmas was the best ever, with presents galore, lots of games and an amazing Christmas dinner. Snow had even fallen thick over Thistlewick.

Stormy Cliff had received the finest of renovations and the treasure hadn't been wasted. Builders from the mainland had come over to strengthen the walls, replace the windows and fix the roof, and did so in quick time. The interior of the school had received a complete makeover, with decorators re-plastering and painting the walls – the children having voted for the colours. New furniture had been brought in, along with a state of the art adventure playground, the latest computer equipment, up-to-date textbooks and much more. As a finishing touch, all the children had come in to paint a mural covering an entire outside wall of the school, which depicted Ben and Harriet's journey to find the treasure.

Now everything was complete, and to mark the re-opening of the school, Mr Harris, as the new head teacher, was going to give a presentation to all the parents, pupils and villagers of Thistlewick.

'Come on, Ben!' his mother shouted once more.

A number of loud thuds followed, reminiscent of a charging elephant in a small space, but it was only Ben rushing down the stairs and popping his head around the corner, his hair as untamed as ever.

'I swear you're going to break those stairs one day,' said Mr Davies.

'Sorry,' Ben said. 'I nearly forgot my new lucky coin.' He felt the large gold piece in his pocket and smiled. 'Has Mr Traiton's trial happened yet?' This had been something they had all kept a close eye on since his arrest.

'Yes, and as we all thought, he's been sent to prison,' said Mrs Davies, holding out a newspaper, which had arrived that morning. 'There's an article on it in here.'

She handed the newspaper to Harriet, who read the article aloud:

'EXCLUSIVE: THE STORY BEHIND THE TRIAL OF TRAITOR TRAITON

Many of you will never have heard of Thistlewick. It is a small island off the west of our shores and holds only one village. This, however, was the setting for a terrific adventure and the cruel exploits of one Tristan Traiton.

It all started when Traiton, former head teacher of the island's school, Stormy Cliff, instructed two of his pupils, Ben and Harriet Davies, to travel across Thistlewick to uncover treasure for him.

Traiton told them that if they found the treasure he would use it to save Stormy Cliff, which was in desperate need of the money. The children's class teacher, Mr Andrew Harris, was quoted as saying, 'They simply didn't want their school to close so felt they had to help.'

From what we have been told, the children set off on a quite epic adventure and at times a great struggle. They are rumoured to have battled evil creatures, witches and even pirates in the fight for the treasure. Believe this or not, the story grows even darker.

It was quickly noticed that Ben and Harriet were missing from their lessons. On arriving outside Traiton's office to ask him where the children were, Mr Harris and their mother, Mrs Sally Davies, overheard a bone-chilling phone conversation, which revealed that the then head teacher planned to use the treasure not to save Stormy Cliff, but to turn it into a steel works factory.

'He felt it was his right to take the treasure for himself. He wanted it for such evil I cannot comprehend. Thank goodness Mr Harris overheard that conversation,' Thistlewick's vicar said.

As soon as he realised his pupils were in danger, Mr Harris set off to find them while Mrs Davies set up search parties. The teacher came across Ben and Harriet the next day in the forest at the centre of the island and was able to help them cross it. After he explained what Traiton's true plans were, the three of them decided to claim the treasure and take it to the police.

What happened in the cave where the three unlikely explorers discovered the treasure still remains unclear, but it is an undeniable achievement that they found it.

117

With the help of the local fishermen, they took the treasure to the police, who promptly arrested Traiton for conspiracy to pervert the course of education. The evil man was yesterday sentenced to four years' imprisonment on the mainland, away from Thistlewick and Stormy Cliff School.

So what will happen to the treasure now? Thistlewick Island is largely independent from mainland laws and holds many of its own policies. It is the policy of the island that all found treasure should be used for the good of the community, so when the treasure was placed into the hands of the island police, they felt it was only right to give it to Stormy Cliff.

'What better way to use the treasure than to give it to the school,' were the words of Sergeant Radley, head of the island's police force. 'After all, it was two pupils from Stormy Cliff and their teacher who found the treasure and so nobly handed it to us. It is entirely down to them that Tristan Traiton was able to be captured and sent to prison and therefore the treasure seemed the perfect reward.'

Ben and Harriet, along with Mr Harris, who has recently been appointed as the new head teacher at Stormy Cliff School, are now heroes of the island and will 'go down in history' according to the vicar.

Mr Harris only has praise for his fellow adventurers: 'Traiton was right in saying the school was in desperate need of money. He had used most of our funds in planning his evil scheme, leaving the school under threat of closure. Without Ben and Harriet, who knows where we'd be now. I'm very proud of them.'

So it seems like the children really did do what they set out to achieve. They went on an adventure to find treasure to save their school and that is exactly what they have done. The school has been given a complete makeover and, with Tristan Traiton locked up in a prison cell far away, it seems Stormy Cliff and the island are both safe.

The story of the treasure and Stormy Cliff School has now become a widespread news phenomenon but, on a final note, will this newfound fame and recognition change Thistlewick Island?

'Definitely not!' emphasised Mr Harris. 'We have always been a close community and are very proud of our island's history. We don't want anything to change that.''

Ben and Harriet smiled. That wasn't the best account of what had happened but it brought it back to them just what an incredible time they had been through. It was all truly worthwhile. They stared up at their parents, who were also smiling.

'We are so proud of you,' said Mrs Davies, a tear escaping her eye.

'And so lucky to be able to call two very special children our own,' said Mr Davies, putting his arm around his wife. 'And now that I'm back on my feet the future is looking very bright.'

This was one of those moments that all the Davies family would remember forever; they had never felt as close as they were now.

'Come on, we have to go or we really will be late,' said Mrs Davies.

* * *

'Welcome to Stormy Cliff!' Mr Harris said to the audience. 'I will try to keep my speech short – I know how these things can drag on, having sat through a fair few of them myself.'

Everyone chuckled. Seats had been placed in rows around the school hall and were packed with the children, their parents and various other characters from Thistlewick. In fact, most of the islanders had turned up to celebrate the re-opening of Stormy Cliff. Ben and Harriet sat in the first row, surrounded by their classmates. At the front of the hall was a platform on which Mr Harris stood, behind a lectern with the new school emblem engraved on it. Mr Foxsworth stood beside him, looking considerably happier than he had when Mr Traiton was around.

'I'm sure you will know, as the parents, relatives and friends of the children of Stormy Cliff School, that we have been through quite a lot in recent times. But I hope you also know of the efforts that all the children have put in over their Christmas break to make Stormy Cliff a place worth coming to. Thank you, children.' There was a great deal of pride in Mr Harris's voice as he looked around his pupils. 'Of course, none of this would have been possible without the fortunate and timely discovery of the treasure, which has taken all worry away from the school for many years to come. And we all know who we have to thank for that.'

Many of the audience murmured and tried to see Ben and Harriet among them. Mrs Davies started to blush and Mr Davies hugged her tightly.

'We would not be here today,' continued Mr Harris, once the noise had died down, 'if it wasn't for Ben and Harriet Davies, whose courage and bravery in the face of great danger is an example to us all. Without them the treasure would never have been uncovered, and for that we will always be grateful to them. Ben and Harriet, please step up to the front.'

As Ben and Harriet moved out of their seats, they felt the whole audience staring at them, each and every person knowing what had happened on their treasure hunt and viewing them as true heroes. Mr Harris smiled as they climbed the steps to the platform, and when they reached

Mr Foxsworth, he too smiled and presented them each with a large medal.

'Well done,' he said, quietly but genuinely.

The medals shone brightly and had the children's names and an image of Stormy Cliff on them. Ben turned to the audience.

'None of this would have happened if it wasn't for Mr Harris,' he said. Harriet nodded her agreement.

'Three cheers for Harriet, Ben and Mr Harris!' called Mr Sharpe from the back of the hall. Everyone responded loudly. Mr Harris looked quite taken aback; Harriet blushed.

'Thank you,' said Mr Harris, regaining his composure. 'Our thanks must also go to the fishing fleet, Mr Potts, the vicar, who is to marry Miss Susan, and Mr Sharpe, all of whom had a hand in helping to find the treasure. On another note we welcome to our teaching staff Mr Frederick Foxsworth, who has recently become a trainee teacher. Well done, Mr Foxsworth.'

The audience clapped and now it was Mr Foxsworth's turn to blush.

'We hope that Stormy Cliff will be a place that can both educate and entertain, not just the children, but everyone on Thistlewick. This truly is the start of something very special.' Mr Harris paused to look around the hall one last time and couldn't help but smile again. 'So all that is left to do now is to ring the new school bell and officially re-open Stormy Cliff.'

And Ben and Harriet were the first to cheer as the bell rang out from the roof above them, marking the start of a new term and a new era at Stormy Cliff School.

Thistlewick Island in 2008

About the Author

Luke Temple was born in 1988. He spent most of his childhood living with his teacher-parents in prep schools and loved the freedom it gave him. He has always had a close affinity with schools, having had a great education himself, and now thoroughly enjoys working with children. The highlights have been working with the pupils at Hurst College (where his father teaches) on their school plays.

Luke is an environmentalist at heart and enjoys the countryside, especially Cornwall, where he visits every October. This is a big inspiration for him and for the island of Thistlewick.

He has always been creative, regularly coming up with too many ideas for a single mind to handle. Over his short life he has enjoyed a variety of creative past times – writing, drawing, painting and filmmaking – but it's writing that really strikes home and fulfils his creative needs. 'Stormy Cliff' is his first children's book.

Luke eventually wishes to go into teaching, and wants to help promote reading and creative communication for children, as he knows how much it has always helped him to express himself.

The Website

If you'd like to find out more about the world of 'Stormy Cliff', visit the website:

www.stormycliff.co.uk

There you can explore the island of Thistlewick on an interactive map, find out more about the characters and the author, join the Thistlewick Writer's Club and much more!

And now that you've read 'Stormy Cliff', you can get your hands on the hidden treasure!

On the website there is a treasure chest. Find it and click on it to gain access to the hidden treasure. You'll also need to answer the following question to gain access:

What is Mr Traiton's first name?

(Clue: it begins with T and is mentioned several times in this book.)

In the hidden treasure you can uncover even more exciting information about the world of 'Stormy Cliff' and how it was created, as well as games and other things too!

Acknowledgements

My thanks must be shared between many people, and I have a great deal of gratitude for all of them. Suffice to say, without any one of them, 'Stormy Cliff' would not be what it is today.

Firstly, I thank Mum and Dad – you have been more than supportive from start to finish in so many ways and I'm proud to have had you there.

Secondly, I thank Kieran: friend, creative partner, proof-reader (and so much more).

I was very lucky to be granted access to the artistic genius of Jessica Chiba, who very kindly put a lot of energy into the illustrations for 'Stormy Cliff'. Jessicat, thank you!

Thank you to the Pen Press team, who have been friendly and supportive, and thank you to all the teachers who have inspired me throughout my education, especially Mrs (Sue) Price.

Without the blessing of the residents of Thistlewick Island, 'Stormy Cliff' would never have been written, and so I thank them for the trust they have put in me and the support they have given me over time. I feel confident that we can work together on more stories from Thistlewick Island!

And finally, a big thank you to you, the reader, and I hope that you enjoyed 'Stormy Cliff'!

With love,

Luke